Chalf...
DANGER...

'Naturally, if you should marry before you are twenty-one, your husband will inherit the house.'

Marry? What on earth was he talking about? It was all a dream, an extraordinary dream. In a moment I'd wake up in my bedroom in Hampstead, with nothing more serious to worry about than getting my English essay to school that day. But I knew that it really wasn't a dream at all. It was all really happening to me, Laura Cordell – the girl who used to complain that nothing exciting *ever* happened! Now, suddenly, I was the wealthy owner of a spectacular Bel Air mansion.

Also available in the
CHALFONT COLLEGE series

Someone is Watching
Rising Star

Chalfont College 3

Dangerous Summer

LANCE SALWAY

Beaver Books

A Beaver Book
Published by Arrow Books Limited
62-5 Chandos Place, London WC2N 4NW

An imprint of Century Hutchinson Ltd

London Melbourne Sydney Auckland
Johannesburg and agencies throughout the world

First published in 1989 by Piccadilly Press Ltd
Beaver edition 1989

Copyright © Lance Salway, 1989

This book is sold subject to the condition that it shall not, by way of trade or otherwise, be lent, resold, hired out, or otherwise circulated without the publisher's prior consent in any form of binding or cover other than that in which it is published and without a similar condition including this condition being imposed on the subsequent purchaser.

Printed and bound in Great Britain by
Courier International Ltd, Tiptree, Essex

ISBN 0 09 957320 2

CHAPTER ONE

The day my life changed forever began just like any other summer Monday. I woke up later than usual, I remember, and for one awful moment I thought that I'd overslept and was going to be late for school. Then, when I realised that I was on holiday and had been for two weeks now, I sank back on my pillows with relief and listened drowsily to the familiar sounds of morning: faint voices in the kitchen downstairs, the murmur of traffic on Rosslyn Hill, sparrows chattering in the garden outside.

My room was filled with sunlight and I should have been feeling deliriously happy at the thought of the long summer day that stretched ahead. But I wasn't. Instead, I stared gloomily at the ceiling and wondered how on earth I was going to fill all those empty hours. There was always a chance that something exciting would happen, of course, but I didn't hold out much hope. Nothing interesting *ever* happened to me. As things turned out, though, I couldn't have been more wrong!

I stopped feeling sorry for myself after a while and got out of bed and headed for the shower. As I stared at my reflection in the bathroom mirror I wished, not for the first time, that I looked exotic and glamorous like my cousin, Abby. Whenever I told her this, which was often, Abby said that I must be out of my mind – I was so lucky to be the blonde English rose type and, anyway, she'd give her back teeth to have a skin like mine. Now I peered doubtfully at my skin in the mirror. What was the point of having lovely skin if everything else seemed so pale and uninteresting? Gentlemen were supposed to prefer blondes but I'd never seen any evidence of it. Unless you count Jay Hendriksen slobbering all over me at Danny Angeleno's end of term party. Jay Hendriksen was living proof that not all Australians are big, bronzed and beautiful. He was also the world's worst kisser. No, English rose or not, there didn't seem to be any hope for me at all. Not with boys, anyway.

On my way down the stairs I met my aunt coming up, carrying a mug of coffee. She smiled when she saw me. 'I don't know what's happened to Abby. Maybe this will get her moving.'

'She'd better hurry or she'll be late for her rehearsal,' I said, and carried on in the direction of the kitchen. It was all very well for Abby, I thought. She gets coffee in bed as well as an exciting day. Some people have all the luck.

While I waited for the toast to pop up, I went out into the garden. I stood on the patio for a moment, enjoying the sun on my face and the heavy scent of honeysuckle in the air. Then I went back inside to rescue my toast.

Aunt Maxine came in as I was sitting down, and joined me at the table with a cup of coffee. She was looking elegant as always, far too elegant to be anyone's aunt. It's a word that always makes me think of a bespectacled old lady. Maxine thinks so, too, which was why we'd agreed right from the beginning that I would always call her by her first name.

'Abby's overslept,' she said. 'She'll have to hurry if she wants to get to her rehearsal on time.'

I nodded and took a generous mouthful of toast and marmalade. It would serve Abby right if she *was* late.

'And *I'll* be late for *my* rehearsal, if I'm not careful,' my aunt went on. 'Poor Laura, it must be hard for you having two actresses in the family.' She laughed, and then said, 'What have *you* got planned for today? Anything interesting?'

'Nothing special,' I mumbled.

'Darling, I *am* sorry.' She took my hand and held it for a moment. 'I know that you and Abby were planning a trip together this summer, and that her play means that you won't be able to go, after all. You must be feeling wretched about it. But it *is* a big chance for her . . .'

Yes, it was a big chance for Abby. She wanted to be an actress more than anything else in the world and it seemed that all her prayers had been answered when she was offered a part in a summer holiday youth theatre production of *The Merchant of Venice*. The only trouble was that she and I had already planned a trip to France that summer, to visit family friends near Bandol. And after that we were going to wander along the Mediterranean coast to Italy. Abby's play had put a stop to all that, of course. Now, she spent every day rehearsing with her exciting new friends while I sat at home and wondered what to do with myself. It wasn't fair. It wasn't fair at all.

'Did you see that piece about her in the paper last

night?' Maxine said then. 'She's very lucky to have that kind of publicity so early in her career. And,' she lowered her voice confidentially, 'I see that she's got a single red rose in a vase by her bed.' She peered at me mischievously. 'Is there a new boyfriend on the scene?'

I shook my head and buttered a second piece of toast. 'I've no idea,' I said. 'I thought she was still going out with Gary Goldman.'

'Oh no,' Maxine said. 'That's all over. At least, I *think* it is. But you can never tell with Abby.'

No, you can never tell with Abby, I thought glumly. No one could say that about *me*, though. What *did* they say, I wondered? Poor old Laura Cordell. *So* different from her cousin, isn't she? You'd hardly think they were related at all. Abby's so vivacious and popular, no wonder every boy she meets wants to take her out. Laura's a pretty little thing, I suppose, but why can't she make more of an effort?

'Now I really *must* go,' Maxine said, 'or I'll be late too. Bye, darling. See you later.' She turned at the door to blow me a kiss and then she was gone.

I finished my toast and then wondered whether I should treat myself to another piece or not. In the end, I decided against it and settled for an apple instead. After a few minutes I heard the front door bang as Maxine left for her rehearsal.

There was silence for a while and then the sound of frantic footsteps upstairs told me that Abby was out of bed at last. I was in no mood for bright conversation about her play so I took my apple up to my bedroom and shut the door. My aunt had been right: it *was* hard sometimes having two actresses in the family. Even I had to admit, though, that life with Maxine Anderson was exciting and unpredictable most of the time. She is a famous stage actress and I've lived with her and Abby ever since my mother was killed in a car accident when I was ten. Maxine has been like a mother to me ever since, and Abby has always seemed like my own sister. We're almost exactly the same age – Abby's only two months older – and even though we couldn't be more different in looks and character people often assume that we *are* sisters. We get on well together, too – more often than not. It's only when the stage rears its ugly head that tempers begin to fray and life in our peaceful Hampstead house becomes explosive.

It was like that now. Not only was Abby busy with her production for the youth theatre but Maxine was rehearsing a play, too. It was due to open in the West End in a couple of weeks and she was filled with terror at the prospect. She always said that stage fright doesn't get any less the more famous you become but I wouldn't know about that. Despite the fact that my aunt is such a famous actress I've never felt the slightest interest in following in her footsteps and going on the stage myself. It's different with Abby, though. She lives for the theatre and is determined to become a star, come what may. I can't imagine anything I'd like less.

Maxine's husband, Jonathan Sherwood, isn't interested in the theatre either. He works for a company in the City – something to do with stocks and shares and investments, I think – but even though their interests are so different, he and Maxine seem very happy. They have been married for several years; he's her third or fourth husband, I forget which. I like Jonathan a lot: he's calm and sensible and quiet but he can be fun, too. Whenever Maxine and Abby are being more temperamental than usual and their tantrums become too much to bear, we often sneak out of the house together and go to a movie or for a pizza in the Village until it's safe to go home.

Jonathan's always there when any of us need him. I often wish that he was my real father. I can hardly remember my own. We lived in America when I was little, and I have dim memories of a tall man with a loud laugh who read me stories about Brer Rabbit. My parents divorced when I was five and my mother brought me to live in England, so I only saw him once or twice after that when he came over on business trips. He always remembered my birthday, though, and Christmas; expensive presents would arrive without fail, and there'd be telephone calls, too, when I was younger. But it isn't easy to have a conversation with a father you hardly know and can barely remember so the telephone calls stopped after a while. The presents kept coming, though. As the years passed, I thought about my father less and less. My aunt would mention him occasionally – he was very rich, apparently, with a large mansion in Los Angeles – but I wasn't interested. Why should I care about someone who didn't care about me? I was happy enough in my new life with Maxine and Abby and Jonathan. They were all I wanted. And all I ever needed.

I heard Abby bang the door of her bedroom and then

the sound of her footsteps on the stairs. There was silence for a while after that – I guessed she was snatching a quick breakfast – and then I heard the sound of her voice in the hall. I tiptoed onto the landing and peered over the banister. Abby was talking to someone on the phone and I stayed where I was for a moment, listening. It was a dreadful thing to do, I know, but I couldn't help it. Maybe I could find out if she *did* have a new boyfriend or not.

'What does it matter?' Abby seemed to be angry about something. 'You *know* how much it matters, Mel!'

Mel. She was only talking to Mel. I slipped back into my room, my cheeks burning with a mixture of guilt and disappointment. Mel Rosidis was Abby's best friend and one of the nicest people at Chalfont. A few months or so ago someone had tried to kidnap her little brother but she seemed to be getting over the shock with the help of her new boyfriend, a dishy Venezuelan called Anton Something. He'd come to Chalfont School in the middle of the term and caused quite a sensation in our year. Glamorous South Americans are pretty thin on the ground, even at Chalfont. Mel and Anton, Abby and Gary – or whoever her boyfriend was now. Everyone seemed to have someone. Everyone but me.

I wished suddenly that the holidays were over and we were all back at school. Thinking of Abby and Mel and Anton had reminded me how lonely I'd been the last couple of weeks. At least in term time I had company during the day. I didn't really have a special friend but I went around with Rachel Quinn a lot of the time or else in a crowd with Danny Angeleno and Jay and Olivia Strickland. Rachel had landed a glamorous job in Italy for the summer so I wouldn't be seeing her for a while. I didn't know about Danny and the others but I guessed they had gone their separate ways too.

One of the best things about coming to live with Maxine and Jonathan was going with Abby to school at Chalfont. It's a small international school tucked away behind the houses and flats and chestnut trees that edge a quiet street in St John's Wood. If it wasn't for the elegant stone pillars flanking the entrance and the discreet sign beside them that reads 'The Chalfont School', no one would ever guess that there is a school there at all. But, at the end of a long tree-lined drive, there are a couple of spacious playing fields and then the main building, which is Victorian with lots of turrets and stained-glass windows and was once a mansion called Chalfont Grange. The classrooms behind it were added much later and are built mainly of glass which makes them hot in summer and freezing cold in winter. None of this can be seen from the street, though, which is why visitors are always taken by surprise when they come to the school for the first time.

Most of the students at Chalfont are from other countries – Tammy-Ann Ziegler and Gary Goldman are American, for example, and Lee Nelson's father is an ambassador for one of the Caribbean countries, and Jay Hendriksen is Australian – and this makes the school an exciting place to be. The teaching's informal, too, with small classes and a relaxed atmosphere. There are no rules to speak of, and hardly any restrictions at all for the fifth and sixth forms. We all study for the International Baccalaureate, which is recognised by colleges all over the world, and that's why Chalfont is favoured by parents who travel around a good deal and who want their children to have an international education. A lot of show business people send their children there, too, especially those whose work takes them abroad for much of the time. Like Maxine Anderson, for instance. I wished now that it was a Monday morning in term time and that I was walking with Abby up that familiar tree-lined drive to spend forty minutes discussing *Macbeth* with Jim Curtis, who took us for Eng. Lit. I started to work out how many weeks of the holidays were left and then the sound of the front door slamming sent me scurrying to my window to see Abby dashing up the street towards Rosslyn Hill, her chestnut curls dancing in the sunlight as she ran.

I stayed by the window for a while as silence seeped through the house. Before long, our housekeeper, Mrs Hargreaves, would start work and the stillness would be shattered by the moan of the vacuum cleaner. Until then, though, I had the place to myself. Suddenly, I felt chilly in the sunlight and I turned away from the window. This is ridiculous, I told myself firmly. Pull yourself together, Laura. It's a glorious day and all London is waiting to be explored. If excitement won't come to you, then go out and find it.

I remembered Abby talking on the phone to Mel and this gave me an idea. I knew that Rachel Quinn was in Italy but there was bound to be someone else still in town with nothing much to do. Maybe we could do something together, even if it was just browsing round Covent Garden or going to a movie. I headed for the phone downstairs.

There was no reply at all from Olivia Strickland's number. I tried Tara Lenkowsky next but she said that some cousins had just arrived from Israel and she couldn't get away that day. Another time, maybe. I shrugged and put down the receiver. Who should I try next? Not a boy, obviously – I didn't want any of them to think I was making a pass. It would be great to spend a day with Danny Angeleno, though. I liked him more than any other boy at Chalfont. Maybe if I rang his sister – what was her name? Bonnie, that was it. Maybe if I rang Bonnie Angeleno I'd get to talk to Danny. But she'd only think I was mad. And so would he. No, it was best to stick to girl friends. But who? It wasn't worth trying Mel because she'd be fully occupied with Anton and anyway she was Abby's friend, not mine. I sighed. There was nothing else for it. It was Tammy-Ann Ziegler or no one. I gritted my teeth and dialled Tammy-Ann's number. This was really scraping the barrel but I was determined to spend the day with *someone*.

Tammy-Ann was in. 'Why, Laura, I'd just love to!' she squawked when I suggested we spend the day together. 'There's a problem, though.'

'What problem?' I asked.

'I'm off to the States in a week or so and I've just got to find something decent to wear. And gifts for the family, of course.'

'Of course,' I muttered.

'We always try to find something special to take back

to Fort Wayne,' Tammy-Ann burbled on. 'Something the folks there have never seen.'

That shouldn't be difficult, I thought, but I said, 'Well, I'll come and help. I'm full of bright ideas.'

'Fine. Come on over, Laura,' she said. 'Then we'll head for Knightsbridge or someplace.'

Tammy-Ann lived in an expensive apartment block near Regent's Park. It was just round the corner from Chalfont, as it happened, so getting there was no problem. I knew the route like the back of my hand. Mel Rosidis and Anton lived in the building behind Tammy-Ann's – in separate apartments, of course – and I slowed down when I passed their entrance, in the hope that I might see them and delay the start of my day with Tammy-Ann Ziegler.

There's nothing really wrong with Tammy-Ann. In fact, at first sight everything seems right with her. She's tanned and attractive with long honey-blonde hair – she always looks as though she's stepped out of a soft drinks commercial. It's when she opens her mouth that people fall back in horror. Tammy-Ann has the sort of voice that makes a high-speed drill sound melodious. This wouldn't be too bad if she didn't use it so much and if the things she said weren't as snide as they usually are. As I walked up to the entrance of her building, I comforted myself with the thought that a day with Tammy-Ann Ziegler would at least help me count my blessings, if nothing else did.

The day turned out much better than I'd expected. Tammy-Ann's mother insisted that we have coffee and a slice of her home-made angel food cake before setting off and it was pleasant to sit in the Zieglers' comfortable living room while the two of them looked forward to their trip to the States. Tammy-Ann's father was an executive in the London office of an American electronics company but none of the Zieglers liked England much and they lived only for their annual trips home to Fort Wayne, Indiana. This time Tammy-Ann would be travelling on ahead to spend some time with her grandparents in Palm Springs before flying east to rejoin her parents. 'That's why I've got to find some clothes,' she shrilled. 'I haven't got a thing that's suitable for California.'

'Oh, poor you,' I said acidly. Tammy-Ann shot me a suspicious glance so I added hurriedly, 'Still, we're going to have lots of fun replenishing your wardrobe.'

'Yes,' said Tammy-Ann sweetly. 'Maybe *you* should look out for something new, Laura. You sure could do with it.'

Mrs Ziegler insisted that we took a taxi to Knightsbridge, and Tammy-Ann and I spent a contented couple of hours roaming round Harrods before moving on after lunch to the select boutiques in Beauchamp Place. I didn't buy anything at all but Tammy-Ann spent a fortune on swimwear that looked as though it would disintegrate at the slightest touch of water, and on expensive souvenirs of London that she claimed would knock 'em dead in Fort Wayne. We ended the day at the new Meryl Streep movie in a cinema on the King's Road.

It was the rush hour when we came out of the cinema and so it took us ages to find a taxi. Then Tammy-Ann insisted that I have a cup of tea and more cake at her apartment. Thanks to these delays it was getting on for seven by the time I at last arrived home.

I could tell that something was wrong the minute I opened the front door. The house was suspiciously quiet, for one thing, and for another, Maxine came out into the hall as soon as I opened the door. Her eyes were suspiciously moist and her smile was too bright to be genuine.

'Laura, darling,' she said when she saw me. 'We've been wondering where you were . . .'

'I've been out with a friend,' I said, puzzled by her concern. 'I left a note.'

'Yes, I know.' She paused, then, 'Come into the sitting room. I've something to tell you.'

'What's happened?' I said as I followed her into the room. 'What's the matter? Is Abby –'

Maxine shook her head. 'Abby's fine. Sit down, darling. Now, you must be very, very brave. There's been bad news.'

'Bad news?'

'About your father. We had a call from the States an hour ago. I'm afraid he died early today. It was his heart, I believe. It was quite quick and – and painless.'

I stared at her in silence. I didn't feel anything. I didn't feel anything at all.

'I'm so sorry, darling,' Maxine whispered.

'That's okay,' I said. How could I feel sad about a man I didn't know? He was my father but that was just a word. A word that didn't mean anything.

There was a pause, and then my aunt touched my arm

gently. 'There's more,' she said. 'Jessica – that's your father's wife – would like you to go out there to see them.'

'Out there?' I didn't know what she meant. And who was Jessica? She couldn't be my father's wife. My mother was. But she was dead too.

'To California,' Maxine said. 'Los Angeles. Your father's family want you to go out there for a visit. As soon as possible.'

I stared at Maxine in astonishment, and then I began to laugh. 'I'm sorry,' I said at last. 'I'm not hysterical. It's just – '

'It's the shock,' Maxine said firmly. 'Poor darling, it's been a terrible shock for you.'

I nodded, and then I smiled again as I remembered how the day had begun. My life had seemed so dull and empty then. I'd thought that nothing exciting would ever happen to me. But now everything had changed. My father had died and I was going to California. The words of the old song leaped into my mind: 'California, here I come, right back where I started from . . .'

'I'm going to California!' I said to Maxine. She nodded, her eyes bright with tears. 'I'm going to California!' I repeated excitedly. 'Isn't it amazing?'

Chapter Two

I can't remember much about the couple of weeks that followed. I know I spent most of the time wandering about like a zombie, trying to make sense of everything that had happened. And trying to come to terms with everything that was *going* to happen. One minute my life had been calm and orderly and dull and the next I'd discovered I had an American stepmother I'd never seen who wanted me to visit her in Los Angeles, of all places. I'd never been to America and had always longed to go. Maxine went to New York so often to act in plays and films that she didn't think anything of it, and to Chalfont people like Gary Goldman and Tammy-Ann Ziegler flying to the States was no more dramatic than catching the tube to Tottenham Court Road. In fact, my aunt always said that any trip on the Northern Line was a good deal more exciting than a flight across the Atlantic. Now it wouldn't be long before I found that out for myself.

A lot of talking went on, I remember, in between the frantic expeditions to buy clothes suitable for a California summer and to organise a flight reservation and visa. Trying to find something to wear was the hardest part, and I wished more than once that I'd known about my trip when I spent that day out with Tammy-Ann Ziegler. I did think of asking her to join me but I guessed she was already on her way to Palm Springs. Maxine didn't have much time to help as her opening night was only days away, and Abby, of course, hadn't a moment to spare either. So I managed as best I could on my own until, in desperation, I pleaded with my aunt to take a morning off to help me choose.

'But why didn't anyone *tell* me I had a stepmother?' I asked her when we paused for a mid-morning cup of coffee. It was the first opportunity I'd had to talk to her about my father's family. 'I don't know anything about her. No one told me *anything*.'

'Darling, we didn't know ourselves,' Maxine said. 'We had very little contact with your father. All our communications about you were through lawyers and bankers. We hardly ever heard from him direct. Oh, he came over here once or twice years ago but only for brief visits. And he turned up in my dressing room one night when I was doing *Hedda Gabler* on Broadway but those were the only times we met.'

'So he didn't care about me at all,' I said slowly. 'He just wasn't interested.'

Maxine put her arm around me then. 'I think he *did* care but he didn't want to disturb your happiness with us. I used to send snapshots of you every Christmas. I'm sure he cared for you, deep down. But he didn't really know you. After all, your mother left him when you were five and came over here to live. And then there was the accident . . .'

'What was he like?' I asked urgently. 'I don't mean to look at – I've seen photographs. What was he really *like*?'

'I don't know, darling,' Maxine said sadly. 'I hardly knew him. Your mother met and married him in the States and so I didn't set eyes on him until they came over here on their honeymoon. He seemed charming enough, I suppose. But they were never really happy together.'

'And now he has another wife,' I said. 'My stepmother.'

'Yes, Jessica Gordon Cordell. She sounds charming on the phone. They're so looking forward to meeting you.'

'They?'

Maxine frowned slightly. 'The family. Jessica has a son, I believe, from another marriage. Apart from that, I don't know anything about her or the family. I expect there'll be other relatives who'll want to meet you, too.' I must have looked worried then because she went on quickly, 'You'll have a marvellous time, darling. LA's a wonderful place and I'm sure they'll make a great fuss of you.'

I shivered and stared down at my cup. Suddenly I didn't want to go. I wanted everything to be as it was before. I preferred it that way.

'Come on, Laura,' my aunt said briskly. 'We've still got to find you some beachwear. And something grand for the evenings. I'm sure there'll be lots of parties . . .'

I think I began to feel really excited about the trip when I heard that magic word – 'parties'. I had a sudden picture of myself in a crowded Hollywood night-club, dancing with a handsome boy with fair hair and a dazzling smile, and my heart gave a lurch of excitement.

This was the most exciting thing that had ever happened to me, and I wasn't going to waste a single moment of it!

That evening another call came from Los Angeles and this time I was summoned to the phone to speak to my stepmother for the first time. It wasn't a long conversation because we were both nervous, I think, and I can't even remember what Jessica said. But I do recall her low, pleasant voice and how excited I felt when I put the receiver down. I longed more than ever for the day to come when we'd meet face to face.

It was Jonathan who first mentioned the will to me. My memory of those confusing days is hazy now but I can vividly remember walking with him in the garden one evening while he told me that my father had remembered me in his will. Talks with lawyers and accountants were still going on, and none of the details were settled yet because it took time to finalise matters, especially when two different countries were involved. Anyway, I was still under age and didn't need to concern myself with such things. Yet.

I didn't know what on earth Jonathan was talking about. 'Do you mean my father's left me some money?' I asked.

'I've told you, I don't know the details. Their lawyers are talking to ours. It all takes time.'

'When will we know?'

He coughed nervously. 'I expect they'll tell you more when you get to Los Angeles. But don't worry about it, Laura. Just concentrate on having a wonderful time.'

I grinned at him. 'Oh, I'm going to,' I said. 'I can hardly wait.'

There are other memories, too. The first night of Maxine's play, for instance, and her marvellous performance as a middle-aged woman falling in love with a younger man and wondering whether or not to leave her husband. The play itself wasn't up to much but Maxine was enchanting and glamorous and I was so proud of her that night. Jonathan and I had seats in the stalls, next to Abby and a good-looking boy who was in her play and whose name was Adam something or other. We all cheered and stamped at the end, and then crowded into Maxine's dressing room to tell her how wonderful she was. There was a party afterwards at someone's house but I didn't go. Instead, Jonathan took me home in a taxi before going back to join the others.

And then, the night before I was due to leave, I remember Abby coming into my room and how we stayed up for hours, just talking. It was a long time since we'd had a heart-to-heart, and we chatted about everything under the sun but mainly about Abby's play and her complicated love life. She was involved with a boy called Ricky but they'd had a row about something and that was why she'd brought Adam to the play instead. Adam was keen on her, apparently, but she didn't know whether he was in love with her or with her famous mother and what did I think she should do? I can't remember what I said but I know I told her that I was sorry I wouldn't be there to see her play but that I'd definitely be around for the next one.

'I do envy you going to LA,' Abby sighed at last. 'Promise to write and tell me everything. And take lots of pictures. I want to know what everyone looks like.'

'Thanks for reminding me,' I said. 'I'd forgotten all about my camera.' I fished it out of a drawer and popped it into the suitcase that I'd been packing and re-packing for the past week.

'Why don't you go and visit my father while you're there?' Abby said excitedly. 'I'm sure he'll be pleased to see you. I'll give you his number. He lives in Brentwood, I think.'

'But he won't remember who I am,' I protested. Abby's father is Billy Day, the film actor. He comes to London from time to time and swamps Abby with expensive presents before flying off again into the sunset.

'Don't be stupid,' Abby said. 'Of course he'll remember you.' Then she laughed. 'Isn't it odd? Here we are, a cosy family of four, and we've all got different surnames!'

'That's because we've all got such complicated and mysterious pasts,' I said. 'At least you know all about your family. I'm only just beginning to find out about mine.'

Abby reached out and took my hand. 'I hope it all works out okay for you, Laura,' she said gently. 'You deserve some good luck for a change.'

I smiled at her, and nodded. 'It's going to be exciting,' I said. 'And fun, too.'

'Maybe you'll fall in love with some gorgeous surfer who'll whisk you off to fame and fortune,' Abby said, her eyes alight with mischief.

'Fall in love? Me? You *must* be joking!' I smiled back at her, pretending to be amused too. But it was no joke, believe me. 'I should be so lucky,' I said lightly. 'You know *my* luck with boys. The hunks turn and run and I get left with nerds like Jay Hendriksen.'

'That's going to change,' Abby said firmly. 'It's all going to be different from now on, just you wait and see.'

'Is it?' I wasn't convinced.

'Of course,' Abby went on. 'I know it will.'

'Okay,' I said. 'I believe you.' And then we started to talk about something else. Later on, after she'd gone back to her own room, I remembered what Abby had said. Maybe she was right. Maybe things were going to change for me. Maybe I *would* meet someone in California. After all, anything might happen there. Anything at all.

And then, suddenly, it was the morning of my flight, a blur of last minute packing, tearful goodbyes, and Jonathan driving me to Heathrow and waving me cheerfully through to the departure lounge. 'Bye, Laura,' he said. 'Phone us when you get there. But for God's sake remember the time difference. They're eight hours behind us.'

I gulped and said, 'I'll remember. See you in a few weeks.'

He kissed me lightly on the cheek, and I turned and walked away. I didn't feel sad or excited. I just felt sick.

The sick feeling stayed with me all the way onto the plane until at last the great steel monster had groaned its way into the sky and I was able to unfasten my seat belt and relax. Then I began to feel better: I could forget all about London and Maxine and Abby for a while and concentrate on the days ahead. I should have felt scared, I suppose. After all, I was flying all by myself to a country I'd never visited to stay with people I'd never met. What if I hated California? And what about my father's family? I might take an instant dislike to them, and they might do the same to me. What then? I grinned to myself, and shrugged. One of the last things Maxine had said to me that morning was, 'Don't forget, you can call us at any time.' I'd nodded, and she went on, 'We're always here if you should need us. And you can come home whenever you want to. You've got your return ticket. You can come home any time, Laura. Any time at all.' Then she'd given a high nervous laugh and hugged me close. 'Off you go,' she'd said huskily after a while. 'Have a good time, darling.'

I smiled to myself at the memory and shut my eyes. Then I heard a voice and opened them almost at once. An air hostess with a smile two feet wide was leaning over the empty seat next to me and asking if I wanted anything to drink before lunch. I ordered a Coke and settled back comfortably in my seat. I was going to enjoy myself from now on, come what may.

The journey seemed to last forever. As the plane droned on through the day, I drifted into a doze and then shot awake with a start, wondering where I was. I felt tired and a little irritable so I got to my feet and made my way towards the washroom. I had only gone a few feet when I stopped dead in surprise. Seated a few rows back from me, her face buried in a copy of the in-flight magazine, was Tammy-Ann Ziegler.

I wasn't sure what to do. I could sneak past and hope

that she wouldn't look up and notice me, or else I could breeze up to her and say, 'Hi, Tammy-Ann, fancy meeting you here!' In the end, I decided that there was little point in trying to hide as she would probably notice me later in the flight. No, the best thing to do was make the first move.

I'm glad that I did. It was worth it, just to see the expression on Tammy-Ann's face when she looked up and saw me grinning down at her. I'd never before seen Tammy-Ann at a loss for words but she was struck dumb for a full minute when she saw me that day. 'Lau – Laura,' she gulped after a while. 'What are – what are *you* doing here?'

'Same as you, I expect,' I said. 'Flying to LA.'

There was an empty seat next to Tammy-Ann and I flopped into it to explain the situation to her. She was suitably impressed, and I stayed where I was for a while to make the most of the situation, and to enjoy Tammy-Ann's astonishment.

'Pity we won't be able to see each other while you're over there,' she squawked at last. 'My grandfather's meeting me at LAX and we're driving straight to Palm Springs. Who's meeting *you*, Laura?'

I shrugged. 'My stepmother, I suppose. I don't know. They said they'd recognise me from the last photographs my aunt sent to my father.'

'How *weird*!' shrilled Tammy-Ann cheerfully. 'I mean, you might have coloured your hair, or anything. You might look completely different by now and they'd never recognise you. You could miss each other completely.'

I gave Tammy-Ann a sharp look. She had clearly got over her surprise and was back to her familiar stupid self. 'Grow up, Tammy-Ann,' I said wearily. 'I know the address. Somewhere in Bel Air. I could phone them, or get a cab. I'm not helpless.'

'They live in Bel Air? Wow!' Tammy-Ann was clearly impressed by this but it meant nothing to me and I said so irritably. I was now beginning to regret talking to her in the first place. It would have been better to have sneaked past her and kept my head down for the rest of the flight. On the other hand, it was going to be a long boring trip and she *would* be company. Of a sort.

'I was on my way to the washroom,' I said, and got to my feet. 'See you later, Tammy-Ann.' I pushed past her but I must have tripped over a bag or something because I suddenly lost my balance and half-fell into the aisle, crashing into someone who was passing by. Then someone let out a frenzied yell as my heel ground into his foot, and I looked up in embarrassment to find a pair of furious hazel eyes glaring down at me.

'I – I'm terribly sorry,' I blurted out. 'I lost my balance. I didn't mean – '

I was standing upright again by this time and I saw that I had collided with a tall boy of about my own age, with fair curly hair, and freckles scattered over a snub nose. His tanned face was twisted with pain.

'Why can't you look where you're going?' he groaned. He was an American by the sound of it. 'Are you always this clumsy or have I done something to annoy you?'

I drew myself up to my full height and shot him a glare

that could shatter concrete. The boy didn't seem impressed. Instead, he muttered, 'Just clear out of my way, will you?' And he limped past me.

I stared after him, my mouth hanging open with astonishment. I may have hurt him when I fell but there'd been no call for such rudeness. It had been an accident, after all. I hadn't fallen deliberately.

'What a creep!' Tammy-Ann squawked behind me. 'Pity you didn't get him where it hurts most!'

I shot her a grim smile, and stalked away towards the washroom. My face was burning with anger and humiliation. If that was the way American boys behaved then the sooner I headed home the better.

It took a long time for my anger to subside. When I got back to my own seat I noticed that the boy was sitting across the aisle from me but I ignored him completely and instead buried my nose in one of the glossy fashion magazines that Abby had pushed into my hands when I left home. After that I dozed a little and tried to picture what the next few days would be like. Would I like my stepmother? Would she like me?

I went back to talk to Tammy-Ann later on, after yet another meal had been brought round by the stewardess with two hundred teeth. And then I dozed again, as the plane moaned endlessly on.

By the time the announcement came that we were soon to land at Los Angeles International Airport it seemed as though I'd been on that plane all my life. But then I forgot the boredom of the flight and Tammy-Ann and the bad-tempered boy as I fastened my seat belt and peered out of the window, anxious for my first sight of

California. I couldn't see anything at first, just brilliant blue sky hung with puffs of cotton-wool cloud. Then the plane began to circle and descend, and I saw blue-green sea edged with gleaming beach, barren hills, block after block of houses stretching into haze, freeways crowded with cars like ants on loops of spaghetti. And then I sat back and braced myself as the huge plane thundered to a halt on the runway. We had landed. I was there. I was in California.

CHAPTER THREE

I couldn't wait to get off the plane. As soon as the other passengers began to move towards the exit, I gathered my things together and stood up. I stepped into the aisle and then came suddenly face to face with the fair boy with the freckles who'd been so rude earlier on. Now that he was no longer snarling with pain I could see how good-looking he was. He gave me a sheepish grin and opened his mouth to say something but I looked quickly away and followed the other passengers out of the plane. The boy may have been handsome but I hadn't forgotten how unpleasant he'd been to me. I wasn't going to give him the satisfaction of an apology.

It seemed to take hours to get through customs and immigration but I didn't really care. I hoped that it would take forever. The familiar sick feeling had returned: I was nervous about meeting Jessica and the others, and scared of what I might find. I looked round for Tammy-Ann while I was waiting to claim my luggage, in the hope that the sight of a familiar face might reassure me, but she was nowhere to be seen.

I came to a dead stop at last in the arrivals area, confused by the noise and the crowds. I looked round wildly, a nervous grin fixed on my face, hoping to see someone I recognised but realising that I didn't know a single person there. And then I felt a gentle tap on my shoulder and I swung round to find myself looking into the smiling face of a tall dark-haired young man in sunglasses.

'Hi!' he said. 'You must be Laura. You're a lot prettier than your photographs.'

I felt my face reddening and knew that I was looking anything but pretty at that moment. I felt tired and grubby and I wanted to turn round and go straight home. I said weakly, 'Yes, I'm Laura Cordell but – '

'Jessica couldn't make it so she sent me instead,' the young man said. He took off his sunglasses, revealing startling blue eyes that stared curiously into mine. I looked at him blankly and he went on, 'Oh, I'm sorry. You don't know who I am. Todd Gordon, Jessica's son. I guess we're almost related.' He looked much younger without the glasses – I guessed that he was about four years older than I was.

I smiled at him weakly and said, 'Oh yes, of course.'

'Here, I'll take your bags,' Todd said. 'Sam's waiting outside with the limo. We'll be back at Saxonwood in no time at all.'

I must have looked as bewildered as I felt because Todd laughed and said, 'Sam's our driver. I'd have come in my Peugeot but Jessica insisted on the Cadillac. Much more class. And only Sam's allowed to drive *that*.'

I nodded. 'And Saxonwood?'

Todd raised his eyebrows in surprise. 'That's the house. The name of the house. Surely you know *that*? You lived there as a kid, didn't you?'

'I can't remember,' I said. 'And I don't know anything

about you or Jessica. I didn't even know you existed until a couple of weeks ago.'

Todd gave me a slow, charming smile. 'Then you've sure got a lot to learn. Come on, let's get out of here.' And he picked up my bags and began to thread his way through the crowd.

We paused for a moment when at last we emerged from the terminal building. I was uncomfortably aware of a blast of intense heat, and brilliant sunlight bouncing off steel and glass, and then an enormous car with tinted windows appeared from nowhere as if by magic and a sallow man in uniform took my bags as Todd ushered me into the back seat.

I sank back and closed my eyes briefly as the car slid away from the kerb. After the heat outside, the car seemed refreshingly cool and I guessed that it was air-conditioned.

'How was the flight?' Todd was sitting beside me; he looked cool and sophisticated in an open-necked shirt and pale blue chinos.

'Very, very long,' I said. 'I thought it would never end.'

'Well, it's a long way,' he said. 'Have you ever been back to the States since – since – '

'Since the divorce? No, never. And I can't remember much about living here. I was only five when we left for England, and I've never been back.' I was beginning to feel more relaxed and cheerful, and I grinned at Todd as I said, 'There's so much that I want to see. All the places I've only read about. Hollywood and Disneyland and Malibu – '

'Verna's got a beach house at Malibu,' Todd said. 'Maybe she'll take you there.'

'Who's Verna?' I asked.

Todd looked at me sharply. '*Surely* you know who –' Then, when he saw my puzzled expression, he said, 'No, I guess you don't. Verna's your aunt. Your father's elder sister.'

I gaped at him like a stranded goldfish. 'My – aunt?'

Todd nodded. 'They never told you, huh?'

I shook my head. 'I thought I only had one aunt. In London. My aunt Maxine.'

'Maxine Anderson? Yes, they told me about her. I've seen her in movies. Verna used to be in movies too, as Verna Travis. Some coincidence.'

'Some coincidence,' I echoed dully. 'You were right, Todd. I've certainly got a lot to learn.'

I looked out of the window. We were now driving in a stream of fast-moving traffic along a freeway that soared above blocks of small houses that stretched away on each side as far as the eye could see. A blue-gold haze hung over the city. Far to the right I glimpsed a cluster of much taller buildings looming over the surrounding plain of houses.

'That's downtown,' Todd said, following my gaze. 'We're on the San Diego Freeway now. The smog's not too bad today. When it's really clear you can see the mountains.'

I turned to smile at him and then I caught sight of the driver in the rear-view mirror. Sam was staring straight at me, his eyes cold and hard. My stomach gave a lurch and I looked quickly away. There was something about Sam that I didn't like. And I didn't think he liked me.

'Tell me about yourself,' I said brightly to Todd. 'I don't know anything about you.'

'There's not much to tell,' he said. 'My father's dead. Jessica married *your* father about eight years ago and we both moved into Saxonwood. I'm twenty years old, I've just finished my junior year at UCLA, and my favourite colour is blue. What else do you want to know?'

'What's your mother like?'

'Jessica? Well, let's just say that she's the kind of mother who hates being called "mom". You'll see for yourself soon enough.'

I wanted to ask Todd about my father but I decided to wait. There'd be plenty of time for questions in the days that lay ahead. I looked out of the window again as the car left the freeway at an interchange and turned right to join another stream of traffic.

'Santa Monica Boulevard,' Todd said, and then a little later, 'Beverly Glen,' as we made a left turn. I gaped at the gleaming cars and buildings, at the tall skinny palms and lacy eucalyptus trees that rose above the houses. Everything seemed bright and colourful and larger-than-life.

The car swung left along a wide road edged with grass and flowers and spacious houses. 'The university's coming up on the left,' Todd said. Then the car made another right turn and then a left and we began to drive along a series of twisting roads. Flowering bushes and trees lined the roadsides and every now and then I caught glimpses of huge white-walled houses behind impressive gates and, in the distance, smoky-green hillsides rising to meet a brilliant blue sky.

Then, at last, the car paused outside a pair of steel gates. The roadside was lined with dense large-leafed shrubs and I couldn't see the house behind them, just a security camera mounted on a brick pillar. I expected Sam to get out of the car to open the gates but he stayed where he was. And then the gates swung open by themselves and the car slid past them and up a long drive lined with immaculate green lawns. We came to the top of a rise and I gasped as I saw the house that lay ahead.

'That's it,' Todd said cheerfully. 'There's Saxonwood. Welcome to the old homestead, cousin Laura.'

'I'm not your cousin,' I said quickly. 'We're not related.'

I didn't look at Todd when I said that because I couldn't keep my eyes off the house. It was enormous, but I had expected the house to be large. What I had not expected was a building that looked like a huge Elizabethan manor house, with diamond-paned windows and half-timbered gables. But it was a Hollywood version of Tudor architecture: it looked like a spectacular film set. All the same, if it hadn't been for the purple bougainvillea climbing over the windows, and the brilliant hibiscus and oleander bushes clustered beneath them, then the house wouldn't have seemed out of place in Hertfordshire. It was only when I got out of the car and felt again the blaze of sunlight on my face that I realised that there was nothing English about Saxonwood. Nothing at all.

Todd opened the front door and ushered me into a

cool panelled hall. He followed me, and Sam came in behind with my luggage. A wide staircase led from the hall to the floor above and, ahead of me, open double doors led into an enormous drawing room. Further on, French windows opened out onto more vivid green lawns and I caught a glimpse of something blue that could only be the water in a swimming pool.

There was a sudden movement on the stairs above me, and a quiet voice said, 'Laura. Welcome to Saxonwood.'

I looked up. A woman was standing on the stairs, smiling down at me. She looked about thirty years old but that was because the light in the hall was dim. As she came down the stairs towards me, I could see that she was really much older, and that the immaculate dark hair, willowy figure, and simple but expensive white silk dress were all carefully designed to give an impression of youth.

I said, 'You must be – '

'I'm Jessica,' she said quickly, and she put a slim tanned arm around me and kissed me on the cheek. I didn't return the caress. Apart from anything else, I was terrified of disturbing the careful make-up. 'We're so glad you could make it,' she went on. Her voice was low and husky, and I wondered if she always spoke like that or if it was put on for effect, like the make-up and the dress. 'You must be exhausted. Let me show you straight to your room and you can freshen up. After that we can really get to know each other properly.'

I remembered the flash of blue water in the garden

beyond, and I said impulsively, 'What I'd like more than anything else is a swim.'

Jessica's eyes widened in surprise and then she shrugged. 'Why not? The pool's there to be used.'

'I'll join you,' Todd said.

Jessica shot him a sharp glance, and I wondered why. Then she led the way back up the stairs, along yards of cool carpeted corridor. Sam followed behind us with my bags. At last Jessica opened a door and said, 'We thought you'd like *this* room. It looks over the pool and has a good view of the mountains. I'll leave you to freshen up now. We'll be downstairs.' She paused at the doorway. 'I hope you'll be happy with us, Laura. We're delighted to see you.' She gave me a dazzling smile and then closed the door behind her.

The room was charming, with a bed like a small four-poster, hung with floral chintz. There was a bathroom leading off it, and French windows which opened onto a balcony. I stepped outside. Below me, velvet lawns sloped down to a large swimming pool. Beyond that, a dense thicket of flowering shrubs and trees shielded the garden from the property next door. If there *was* a property next door – it was impossible to tell. Horse-chestnut and eucalyptus trees rose above the bushes and I could see in the distance a rocky hillside, dotted with scrub and creepers. Overhead loomed the radiant sky; I had only ever seen such a dense unnatural blue on picture postcards before.

I opened my case and found my new swimsuit. Then I quickly changed, checked my face and hair in the dressing table mirror, and headed back downstairs. I had to concentrate to find my way back to the staircase; compared with this spacious mansion, our house in Hampstead was a rabbit hutch. At last I regained the hall and wandered through the huge dim drawing room out into the sunlight. There was a terrace beyond the French windows, shaded by a pergola hung with bougainvillea and wisteria. Beneath it, Jessica and Todd were lounging in comfortable chairs. Todd had changed into swimming shorts and the sight of his firm tanned body reminded me how white and flabby I must look in comparison.

Jessica must have guessed my thoughts for she said, 'Don't worry, you'll soon have a healthy California tan, Laura. But take it easy at first, won't you? The sun can be dangerous.'

'I'll be careful,' I said. 'I just want a quick swim to freshen up.'

I walked away towards the pool, conscious of their eyes on me, and then I forgot all about them as I slipped into the glittering cool water. I wasn't a very confident swimmer and I hoped that no one would laugh at my clumsiness in the water.

Todd joined me there after a while and we splashed about for ten minutes or so. And then we clambered out and lay on the poolside to dry off. After that we went back to join Jessica. There was someone else with her now, a much older woman with far too much make-up and sleek blonde hair that looked natural but probably wasn't. She held out her hands to me as I approached, and smiled. 'Laura,' she said. 'At last.' And then, because I must have looked bewildered, she added, 'I'm your Aunt Verna.'

I didn't say much but then I didn't have to. I sat down with the others and enjoyed a tall glass of iced fruit juice while Verna rattled on about how sweet I looked and wasn't I the spitting image of my poor mother and how she couldn't for the life of her imagine why my father hadn't invited me to Saxonwood while he was alive.

'I'm sorry,' I said when Verna paused for breath. 'I'm afraid I just can't keep my eyes open. It's jet lag, I suppose. I know it's only about four o'clock here but my body tells me it's really one in the morning. I wonder if – '

'Oh, you poor darling,' Verna cooed. 'Here am I boring you to death with my memories and all you want to do is sleep. Why don't you go upstairs and take a nap? Then you'll be fresh for the evening.'

'Yes, I think I will, if you don't mind,' I said, and got unsteadily to my feet.

'Of course we don't mind,' Jessica said. 'We'll see you again at dinner. I thought we'd eat at home. Todd was all for rushing you out to Beverly Hills but I put my foot down. We want you at home on your first evening with us.'

I smiled weakly at her and headed for the house.

'I'll see you to your room,' Verna called after me, and added, 'No, I insist,' when I protested that I could find my own way, thank you very much.

As it turned out, I couldn't remember which room it was so I was glad of Verna's company. I just wished that she'd stop talking.

'Well, here you are,' she said brightly when we reached my door. 'It takes time to find your way around this place but you'll soon get the hang of it.'

'It's a beautiful house,' I said.

'Yes,' Verna said. 'It *is* beautiful. And to think it's all yours. What could Laurence have been thinking of?'

I stared at her for a moment, wondering what on earth she meant, and then she smiled brightly and said, 'Sleep well, dear. We'll have a long talk when you've recovered from your trip. We've got *so* much to catch up on, haven't we?'

When Verna had gone, I quickly undressed and collapsed on the bed. I had never been so tired in all my life but I didn't fall asleep right away. I think I was too exhausted to sleep, if that's possible. After a while, though, I found my eyelids growing heavier as sleep slowly claimed me. And then, as if in a dream, I heard faint voices outside the window. People were talking in the garden. Todd and Jessica. I could only hear snatches of their conversation but I was too tired to get out of bed and listen properly. The words drifted into the room on the slight breeze that gently stirred the curtains. I heard Todd say, 'I don't like it . . .' followed by a mumble from Jessica. And then he said, 'She's got to go. We've got to get rid of her.'

I opened my eyes in shock. Were they talking about me? I was wide awake now. I stayed on the bed, hoping that I'd been dreaming, that I'd only imagined Todd's words. There was a pause, and then I heard Jessica say, 'She's a danger to . . .' The rest of her sentence was lost, and so was the beginning of Todd's reply. I heard him say, '. . . and if she decides . . . *anything* could happen . . .' There was a mumble of voices then and I could hear nothing clearly. Then Jessica said, 'There's nothing else for it, we'll have to stop her . . .'

Outside, the sun still blazed from a clear blue sky. But I felt suddenly very cold. And very frightened.

Chapter Four

By the time I woke up, the conversation I'd overheard seemed little more than a bad dream. I'd been so exhausted after the flight and so bewildered by my new surroundings that it was hardly surprising that I should start to imagine things. I must have fallen asleep after the voices died away because the next thing I remember was a tapping at the bedroom door and a shy young Oriental-looking woman in a black and white maid's uniform coming in to tell me that dinner would be served in an hour's time. I smiled my thanks and leaped off the bed and into the bathroom for a shower. Then I quickly unpacked my bags and chose a pair of cool baggy trousers and a blue and ivory striped top to wear that evening, praying that no one would notice the creases.

The family were waiting for me in the drawing room when I at last went downstairs. It took me some time to locate them; there were at least three other reception rooms on the ground floor, each with different colour schemes and furnished with deep comfortable chairs. I also discovered a room that was lined with floor-to-ceiling bookshelves. I learned later that this was called 'the library', although I never saw anyone reading there.

I found it hard at first to face Jessica and Todd. Were they really plotting to get rid of me? And if so, why? If they didn't want me in the house, then why had Jessica invited me in the first place? It didn't make sense. But they both behaved perfectly normally during dinner. Aunt Verna and Todd did most of the talking, mainly about their plans for my stay in Los Angeles; Jessica said little. By the time we left the table to have coffee in yet another elegant sitting room, I was convinced that my fears were groundless. I was still feeling drained and exhausted, so I excused myself after a while and returned to the calm and comfort of my bedroom.

I awoke next morning feeling rested and much more cheerful. Sunlight was streaming into my room and I lay in bed for a while, looking forward to the day ahead. I was in California! There was so much to do and so much to see – I could hardly wait to start!

After a while, there was a tap at the door and the smiling maid came in with a tall glass of fruit juice and a pot of coffee. She asked me if I wanted breakfast in my room or whether I preferred to join the others on the terrace. I told her that I'd eat downstairs and then she asked if I had any clothes that needed washing or pressing. After she'd gone, I grinned to myself with glee. If only Abby could see me now!

Todd had already finished breakfast by the time I arrived downstairs and so I only had Verna for company. Jessica, it seemed, always took breakfast in her room.

'Ah, Laura!' Verna said when she saw me. 'I hope you slept well, dear.'

I told her that I had, and she went on breezily, 'Now, I'm going to keep you all to myself today. There's so much I want to show you. *And* so much to talk about. It's high time I got to know my beautiful new niece.'

'I – I really don't want to do too much today,' I said. 'I'm still feeling rather tired. And I'll be here for a month at least so I've plenty of time for sightseeing.'

'Oh, I'm not planning much for today, dear,' Verna said. 'I thought lunch at the Beverly Wilshire first and then a short drive maybe. Nothing too energetic.' She laughed roguishly. 'I like a quiet life, believe me.'

A different maid appeared then and asked what I'd like for breakfast. I ordered fruit juice, waffles and coffee, and marvelled yet again at the luxury of life at Saxonwood. I asked Verna how large a staff worked in the house and she told me that there were about six altogether, including the cook. And Sam the chauffeur, of course.

'Now then, if you'll excuse me, Laura,' she said at last, 'I've got one or two things to see to. If you can amuse yourself here this morning, we'll set off for lunch at about twelve-thirty.'

I remembered the tempting cool water of the swimming pool and assured Verna that I'd have no difficulty in entertaining myself for an hour or two. And then I asked if I could use the telephone – I had an important call to make.

'Darling, how are you? How was the trip?' Maxine said when she answered the phone, and then I heard her calling out to Abby and Jonathan and I had to say a few words to each of them before she came back on the line, full of questions about the journey and Saxonwood and Jessica. I didn't tell her anything about yesterday's mysterious conversation, of course; I just said that I was fine and the house was beautiful and Jessica was charming and why hadn't anyone told me about Aunt Verna? And then we said goodbye.

I felt a stab of homesickness as I put down the receiver and thought of the house in Hampstead. Jonathan would just have arrived home from the City and be sprawled in front of the television in the den, a gin and tonic in one hand and the evening paper in the other. Abby would be thinking about an evening out with Ricky or Adam or whoever, and Maxine would be getting ready to leave for the theatre to give another performance of her play. Life at home seemed peaceful and normal and I felt a sudden longing to be there too. Then I glanced out of the window at the sundrenched green lawns and brilliant flowers and told myself not to be so stupid. Pull yourself together, Laura. Here you are, leading a life of luxury, with California waiting to be explored and all you can do is wish yourself back home. Abby and Rachel and Mel and the others would give anything to change places with you. So stop acting like a prize klutz and enjoy yourself, for God's sake! I decided to take my own advice, and wandered outside to explore the grounds.

There seemed to be no end to the gardens at Saxonwood. From the house itself, smooth green lawns stretched forever, broken up by clusters of brilliant hibiscus and crimson camellias. Wisteria, bougainvillea and climbing roses clung to the house itself, and I glimpsed mimosa and yellow jasmine and groups of red and gold trumpet-shaped lilies in beds beyond the swimming pool. As I walked slowly across the lawns, I felt a welcome touch of moisture on my face from the concealed sprinklers which bathed the grass and flowers in a constant damp mist. The lawns ended in a shrubbery of rich purple oleanders and other flowering bushes that I didn't recognise, but a path led past them to further lawns beyond and a tennis court fringed by camphor trees dappled with bright red leaves. Beyond them, pepper trees, palms, and shaggy eucalyptus trees with bark like moonlight rose to meet the brilliant blue sky.

I turned back then and retraced my steps through the shrubbery. I paused when I came in sight of the house again, astonished by its size, by the rambling roofs and countless windows, and by the strange contrast of purple bougainvillea and Tudor gables. The sun glared down on the unreal house like harsh stage lighting on a garish pantomime set.

There was a summer house nearby in the shape of a Greek temple and I sat down on a stone seat there to look at the house more closely. As I watched, Aunt Verna came outside and paused for a moment as she looked round the garden. Then she caught sight of me and walked in my direction across the grass.

'You've been admiring the garden, I see,' she said as she sat down beside me. 'Beautiful, isn't it?'

'Yes,' I agreed. 'And the house is – is wonderful too.'

'I know,' she said gently. 'I was born here, you know, and so was your father. I've lived here all my life except for a couple of years when I was married. Laurence, your father, loved the house as much as I do. So he didn't mind my staying on when he married your mother. And then Jessica came along.' She turned to look at me. 'You spent your first four years here. Don't you remember it at all?'

I shook my head. 'No, I don't.'

'You were named after your father, you know,' Verna went on dreamily. 'Laurence, Laura. We miss him very much. His heart had been troubling him for years, of course, but we didn't expect . . . He was only fifty-six years old. Of course he married late – he was getting on for forty when he met your mother.' She paused, and I saw that her eyes were filled with tears. 'Poor Laurence. My poor little brother.'

'They tell me you're an actress,' I said loudly, trying to change the subject. 'My other aunt's an actress too. Maxine.'

Verna gave an embarrassed laugh. 'Oh, I'm not in the same class as Maxine Anderson. I was in movies for a while, sure. Always below the title, though. I was never really a star.'

'I wonder if I ever saw you,' I said.

'Oh, I expect so,' she said sadly, her gaze far away. 'They show my old movies on TV sometimes. I'm usually Doris Day's best friend. And I played Elvis Presley's mother once.'

'Tell me about him,' I said excitedly. 'What was he like?'

Verna gave me a vague look. 'Oh, he was a pleasant enough young man. Very polite.' She fell silent then, staring at the house but without really seeing it.

'I think I'll have a quick swim before we go out,' I said at last, standing up.

Verna smiled. 'Don't expect me to join you,' she said.

We walked towards the house together. As we stepped onto the terrace, the French doors opened and Jessica appeared, looking immaculate in caramel trousers and a crisp cream shirt, with a discreet glint of gold at her neck and wrists.

'Ah, there you are, Laura,' she said, smiling at me. 'I hope you slept well?' I nodded and she went on, 'I'm sorry Todd's not here to entertain you but he has an appointment downtown with the dentist. Have you – '

'Laura's spending the day with *me*,' Verna said quickly. 'We're having lunch and then going for a drive.'

Jessica's smile faded and she gave Verna a vicious look. 'Well, I hope you both have a nice day. Don't make any dates for tonight, Laura. Dexter and Ethel Shannon are dying to meet you and they've invited us over for dinner. Not you, I'm afraid, Verna. Just Laura and Todd and me.'

Verna said, 'Well, he's *your* lawyer, not mine.' Then to me, 'I'll see you about twelve-thirty, Laura.'

I nodded, and she bustled away into the house. Jessica watched her go and then turned back to me. 'Dexter Shannon was your father's lawyer, Laura. He handled all Laurence's affairs. He wants to meet you, naturally, but I think he also has one or two business matters to discuss with you.' She smiled then but her eyes were cold. 'They're charming people, you'll like them.'

'I'm sure I will,' I muttered. 'Now, if you'll excuse me –'

'I see you've been admiring the garden,' Jessica said, ignoring my attempt to make a getaway and wandering towards a magnificent oleander bush that grew against the wall of the house. 'I expect a lot of our flowers and trees will be strange to you.'

'I'm afraid so.' I gave a nervous laugh, and wondered why I was feeling suddenly so uneasy.

Jessica stretched out an elegant hand and gently touched one of the fleshy purple blooms. 'Did you know that oleanders are poisonous?' she asked.

I shook my head and she went on, 'Well, they are. I read it somewhere. Or someone told me, I can't remember which. Isn't it strange that something so beautiful can be so deadly?' She stared at me for a moment, her face expressionless, and then she flashed a dazzling smile and said, 'Have a good day with dear Verna. I'll see you tonight,' before turning away and going back into the house.

When she had gone, I stayed where I was for a moment, thinking of all that Jessica had said. The uncertainty and anxiety of the previous day came flooding back and I felt nervous and unsettled. I remembered the conversation that I'd overheard, and I shivered, despite the heat. Then I told myself to stop being so stupid, and ran inside to get changed.

By the time twelve-thirty came, I was feeling refreshed after a leisurely swim and looking forward to seeing something of Los Angeles. I had been hoping that we wouldn't be driven by Sam in the Cadillac, and my luck was in. When I emerged from the house, I found Verna waiting for me at the wheel of a large but rather battered pale-blue convertible.

'I thought we'd go in my old Plymouth,' she said cheerfully when she saw me. 'It always gives the valet at the Wilshire a good laugh.'

I got in beside her and we swooped down the drive, through the impressive gates and along the twisting roads past other imposing briefly-glimpsed mansions. Verna turned out to be a skilful driver and so I was able to relax beside her, enjoying the breeze in my hair but wishing that I had brought sunglasses with me. The sunlight was dazzling and, as we turned into Wilshire Boulevard, I was almost blinded by the glare from chrome and glass and metal.

'There's the LA Country Club,' Verna said after a while. '*We* belong to the Bel Air Club, of course.'

'Of course,' I echoed.

'Not far now,' Verna said as we crossed Santa Monica Boulevard. 'The Beverly Wilshire's just at the bottom of Rodeo Drive. Yes, there it is.'

I had a brief impression of an imposing building with red awnings over the ground floor windows and flags flying over the entrance before we turned and swung into a wide drive behind the hotel and drew to a halt under a glass canopy. We stepped out onto carpet and walked straight into a cool lobby, leaving the car to be parked for us.

We ate in one of the hotel's elegant restaurants and the Plymouth was returned to us by a grinning valet when we emerged under the glass canopy once more.

'Now it's time I showed you some of the sights,' Verna announced as we drove slowly up Rodeo Drive. 'This is the most select shopping area in Los Angeles.'

I stared open-mouthed at the luxury stores and boutiques that we passed, most with names that typified style and wealth: Gucci, Cartier, Van Cleef, Arpels. I decided to come back to Rodeo Drive later in my stay for some leisurely window shopping.

After that, Verna drove along Sunset Boulevard and then turned right and up to Hollywood Boulevard.

'This is the centre of Hollywood,' she said. 'Tacky, isn't it?'

I stared at the cheap novelty and souvenir shops, and at the crowds of tourists flooding the pavement, and I was forced to agree that it *was* disappointing. But we parked the car, just the same, and joined the tourists for a while, ending up outside a cinema that looked like a gigantic Chinese pagoda.

'Mann's Chinese Theatre,' said Verna. 'Take a look at the forecourt. It's the tradition for movie stars to leave their handprints and signatures in wet cement here.'

As I stared down at the familiar names – Marilyn Monroe, Burt Reynolds, Elizabeth Taylor, Paul Newman, even R2D2 and the hoofprints of Gene Autry's horse – I felt a shiver of excitement at being in Hollywood at last.

'We've got time for a quick look at the Hollywood Wax Museum,' Verna said, as she led the way further down the street. I could tell from her flushed cheeks and the brightness in her eyes that she was enjoying the day as much as I was.

We spent half an hour in the museum, looking at the waxwork movie stars and watching trailers of Oscar-winning movies, one of which featured Verna in a supporting rôle. Then we retraced our steps to the car and drove up Highland Avenue to see the Hollywood Bowl, a huge open-air amphitheatre nestling in the Hollywood Hills, before driving back down Franklin Avenue and then up into Griffith Park, an impressive open area of hillside and grass and bridle trails. There was a zoo there and a nature museum as well as a bird sanctuary, tennis courts and even a Greek theatre. But we didn't stop at those. Instead, Verna drove up to the high green-domed Observatory so that I could look out across Los Angeles, at the great wide city sprawling into haze as far as the eye could see.

'You should see this view at night,' Verna said. 'It's out of this world.'

'I will,' I said. 'There's plenty of time.' I kissed her on the cheek and she looked at me in surprise. 'Thanks for a lovely day,' I said.

'You're welcome,' she smiled. 'I've enjoyed making the acquaintance of my English niece.'

Then we returned to the Plymouth and drove slowly back down Sunset Boulevard until at last we reached Stone Canyon and the twisting roads that led from there to Saxonwood.

A couple of hours later I was on my way back again, this time in the Cadillac, with Jessica and Todd in the back seat beside me and Sam, sullen as ever, behind the wheel. Jessica had said that the evening would be informal so I'd changed into khaki cotton trousers with a long-sleeved white T-shirt, and I was carrying a cream cotton-knit sweater, just in case the night should turn chilly. Todd was smart as always in pale yellow trousers and an open-necked shirt but his mother's idea of informality wasn't the same as mine – she was wearing a delicate lace dress that displayed her tan and hair to perfection.

It didn't take long to reach the Shannons' house which turned out to be a large modern glass box perched on stilts high above Coldwater Canyon. Dexter Shannon was a thin solemn man who shook hands with me politely and said that it was great to meet me after all this time. His wife's welcome was more effusive: she greeted me with a hug and insisted that I call her Ethel. Then she ushered me straight into the living room to admire the view.

'What part of London do you come from, Laura?' she asked after I'd complimented her on the house and its setting.

'Hampstead,' I said.

'Is that anywhere near Chelsea? My nephew Jake lives there. His father's been working in London for two years. Jake's over here now on vacation, as it happens, staying with us. I'm sure you'll both have a lot in common. He'll be joining us for dinner, though he'd better hurry up if he's going to make it in time. He's been in Pasadena today, visiting with my brother.'

I smiled politely and then Dexter Shannon came up and asked if he could have a private word with me. He led the way into what appeared to be a study. This room too had a magnificent view of darkening hillside and distant twinkling lights.

Dexter smiled at me as I sat down. 'I won't keep you long, Laura,' he said. Then he gave a little cough and went on, 'Your father was a very wealthy man and, of course, he made provision for you in his will. The details needn't concern you just yet. Your guardian, Mrs – er – '

'Sherwood,' I said. 'Maxine Sherwood.' It seemed odd to call her that; Maxine rarely used her married name.

'That's right, Mrs Sherwood. We'll be dealing with her direct on this matter, of course.' He gave another nervous cough. 'All you need to know at this stage is that your father has left you very well provided for. As well as a generous financial settlement, he has left you the house.'

I couldn't believe my ears. 'You mean, he's left me Saxonwood?'

Dexter Shannon nodded. 'The house will be yours when you reach the age of twenty-one. The property and your share of the remainder of the estate will be held in trust till then. After that, they're yours to do with as you wish.' He peered at me seriously over the top of his gold-rimmed glasses. 'You're a very wealthy young woman, Laura. Or rather, you will be in four years' time. I should also say, though, that if anything happens to you before then – '

'You mean, if I should die?' I asked.

He nodded. 'If that should happen, then your share of the estate and the house go to Jessica. Your father left her a substantial share of the estate, of course, and she has income of her own. Naturally, if you should marry before you are twenty-one, then your husband will inherit.'

Marry? What on earth was he talking about? It was all a dream, an extraordinary dream. In a moment I'd wake up in my bedroom in Hampstead, with nothing more serious to worry about than getting my English essay finished on time and deciding what I was going to wear to school that day. But I knew that it really wasn't a dream at all. It was all really happening to me, Laura Cordell – the girl who used to complain that nothing exciting *ever* happened! Now, suddenly, I was the wealthy owner of a spectacular Bel Air mansion.

I grinned weakly at Dexter Shannon and said, 'I'm afraid it's all come as rather a shock. I'd no idea . . . I mean, I didn't expect – '

'Of course you didn't,' Dexter said. 'Your father was very fond of you, though he didn't show it in recent years.'

'And Saxonwood's mine,' I said slowly. 'It's – it's unbelievable.'

'One of the most valuable pieces of real estate in Bel Air,' he said. 'You're a very lucky young woman.'

There was a knock then, and Ethel Shannon put her head round the door. 'Dinner's ready, you two. We're eating out on the patio. Oh, and Jake's home at last.'

I followed her out of the room in a daze. I felt confused and excited and unhappy, all at the same time. What did it all mean? If only Jonathan were here, and Maxine. They'd explain it all to me, they'd know what to do . . .

As we joined the others outside on the patio, I was aware of Jessica's piercing dark eyes gazing straight into mine, and of Todd coming up to me and whispering, 'And now you know it all, cousin dear,' in a light, amused voice. Then I noticed someone else, a tall young man with fair curly hair and freckles scattered over a snub nose.

'Laura, I want you to meet our nephew,' Ethel said proudly. 'This is Jake Shannon.'

Jake and I stared at each other. 'We've already met,' he said at last, and a sheepish smile spread over his face.

'Yes,' I said huskily. I didn't know whether to laugh out loud or scream with rage. 'We certainly have.'

It was the dishy boy from the plane.

Chapter Five

Jake Shannon and I stared at each other for what seemed like five minutes but was probably only a second or two. And then, as his smile broadened into a mischievous grin, I began to laugh too.

'Where did you two meet?' Mrs Shannon asked. 'And what on earth was so funny about it?'

As we sat down at the table, Jake told the others all about our stormy encounter on the plane, transforming a nasty moment into an amusing anecdote. He didn't tell them how rude he'd been, but then neither did he tell them that I'd cut him dead as we left the plane.

'My, what a coincidence!' Ethel Shannon said. 'Isn't it just amazing how small the world can be?'

'Amazing,' Todd muttered beside me. I guessed from his frosty attitude that he didn't like Jake Shannon, and I wondered why. I didn't care for Jake either but that was because I knew he was a pig.

I didn't eat much during the meal. I had too much to think about. My mind was spinning with all that Dexter Shannon had told me, and the sudden reappearance of Jake had only confused me further. Things were happening much too quickly for my liking but perhaps that's how it was in California. Everything there seemed so unreal: the garish flowers, the dazzling cars, the elaborate houses, the glamorous people, they were all so much larger and brighter than life, just as my inheritance and the meeting with Jake Shannon seemed like unbelievable incidents in a corny old Hollywood movie.

After the meal was over, I wandered away from the others into the garden. The evening was warm and still, apart from the constant shrilling of cicadas, and the air was rich with the scent of jasmine. I stood for a moment, looking out over the valley with its scattering of tiny lights, and then turned to see Jake coming towards me across the grass.

I started to walk back to the house but he caught my arm as I passed and said, 'Hey, not so fast. I want to talk to you.'

I stopped, but I didn't dare look at him. I still couldn't believe that we'd met again so soon after the incident on the plane.

'Don't be mad at me,' he said softly. 'I want to apologise. I know I behaved like a heel on the plane. I was feeling tired and sick and I didn't know what I was saying. I'm sorry. Okay?'

He let go of my arm but I stayed where I was, suddenly aware of his closeness. 'Okay,' I said. 'I forgive you.' Then I gave a nervous laugh. 'And I apologise for stepping on your foot. It really *was* an accident, you know.'

'I know,' Jake said. There was a pause, broken by a sudden burst of laughter from the others on the terrace. 'Look,' he went on quickly, 'I'd like to make it up to you, okay? If you're free tomorrow, maybe we could take a trip someplace.'

'Where?' I asked.

'I dunno. You choose.'

'Disneyland,' I said defiantly. 'I've always wanted to go to Disneyland.'

It was too dark for me to see Jake's face so I couldn't tell how he had reacted to my suggestion. But he laughed and said, 'I haven't been there since I was six. Okay, it's a date. Disneyland it is. I'll pick you up, when? Ten, ten-thirty?'

'Okay,' I said. 'I'll look forward to it.'

'Me too.'

Suddenly I didn't want to get back to the others. Jake Shannon was the only person there who had nothing to do with Saxonwood. My relationship with Jessica and Todd and even Verna had changed now that I knew about the inheritance. I saw now why Jessica seemed so hostile and suspicious, and why Todd kept his distance. Even Verna, for all her friendliness, seemed withdrawn and guarded at times. They had all known about the will, and that Saxonwood was mine. How could I expect them to like me? But why then had Jessica invited me to stay? *Why?*

'I guess we'd better get back to the others.' Jake's voice brought me back to reality.

'I suppose so,' I said. 'I'll see you tomorrow.'

At least I would have a day away from Saxonwood, a day away with someone I could trust. For all his faults, I knew that I'd be safe with Jake Shannon.

The rest of the evening passed pleasantly enough but we didn't stay late. None of us said much on the drive back to Saxonwood; Jessica and Todd now knew that I'd been told about the inheritance but we were all reluctant to talk about it.

Verna was still up when we arrived back at the house. She'd been watching television in the drawing room but she got up when we came in and switched the set off.

'Welcome home,' she said. 'How about a nightcap?'

'Nothing for me,' I said quickly. 'I'm really very tired. I'm still jet lagged, I think.'

'I think I'll go up too,' Jessica said, stifling a languid yawn. 'What are your plans for tomorrow, Laura? We were wondering if you'd like a trip up the coast, to Malibu maybe, and on to Ventura – '

'Jake Shannon's asked me to spend the day with *him*,' I said. 'We're going to – '

'*Jake Shannon?*' Jessica said sharply. She and Todd exchanged glances and she went on, 'But you hardly know him, Laura. And *we* don't know him at all. Are you sure that's a good idea?'

'I don't see why not,' I said. 'I'm sorry, but I'd really no idea you'd anything planned for tomorrow. If I'd known, then I wouldn't have accepted Jake's invitation. I'm sorry but I didn't realise . . .' My voice tailed off and I stared miserably at the floor.

'Never mind, dear,' Verna said, coming up and patting my arm. 'You can go with Jessica and Todd another day. And anyway, I'm sure Jake's a perfectly respectable young man. After all, he's Dexter Shannon's nephew. You go right ahead and have a good time.'

There was an uncomfortable pause and then Todd

said, 'I guess Dexter told you about the will, Laura. How does it feel to be the new owner of Saxonwood?'

There was a sudden shocked silence. After a moment I said weakly, 'I'm – I'm not sure. And anyway, I'm not the owner yet. Not really. I don't know anything about it.'

'It'll all be yours when you're twenty-one,' Todd persisted. He stared at me mockingly. 'What are you going to do then? Throw us out on the street?'

I looked into his startling blue eyes and decided to meet his challenge head on. 'Of course,' I said. 'Anyway, I've no use for a house like this. I don't even live in the States. I'll sell the place as soon as I can.'

'Sell Saxonwood? You can't – ' Verna began, but Jessica interrupted her.

'You don't know what you're talking about, Laura,' she said sharply. 'You're far too young to make a decision of that kind. I suggest you get some sleep now. You've had a long day and I expect you're still tired from your flight.'

'Yes,' I said. 'I – I think you're right. I'm sorry. Goodnight.'

As I closed the drawing room door behind me, I heard Verna say plaintively, 'Did she mean it? Is she really going to sell the – ' But then Jessica interrupted her impatiently again with words I couldn't make out, and I walked quickly away, towards the staircase.

I slept well that night, much to my surprise. I'd fully expected to stay wide awake, thinking of all that happened during the evening. But I didn't – instead, I fell asleep as soon as my head touched the pillow. My sleep wasn't entirely peaceful, though; I remember waking with a start from a dream about Jessica. She was standing under a gigantic oleander bush, and I heard her husky voice cooing, 'Isn't it strange that something so beautiful can be so deadly?'

Breakfast was served on the terrace as usual next morning but there was no one to keep me company. The maid, whose name I now knew to be Maria, told me that Jessica and Verna hadn't yet come down, and that Todd had already left the house. I felt a pang of guilt as I remembered the plans that he and Jessica had made to entertain me that day, then I told myself not to be so crass. If they'd told me earlier then I wouldn't have made a date with Jake. Anyway, I felt uneasy about being in their company, now that I knew the terms of my father's will. Perhaps it would do us all good to spend a day apart.

At ten-thirty Jake arrived to collect me in a fuchsia-coloured Volkswagen 'Beetle'. The car seemed so out of place in the formal surroundings of Saxonwood that I laughed out loud when I saw it. Jake looked hurt at first until I explained that I'd assumed that everyone in Los Angeles drove around in Cadillacs or Ferraris.

'Don't let my Aunt Ethel hear you say that,' he smiled. 'I'll have you know that this automobile's her pride and joy. She only let me borrow it because today's a special occasion. And anyway, it matches the bougainvillea.'

'What's the special occasion?' I asked as I climbed into the car beside him.

Jake gave me a serious look. 'Well, it's not every day

that I get to visit Disneyland in the company of a cute British blonde.'

I looked at him for a moment, unsure whether he was joking or not, and then his hazel eyes lit up and an infectious grin spread over his face.

'Not so much of the cute,' I said, pretending to be offended.

'It's a compliment!' he protested.

'Okay, I believe you,' I said. 'Now, are we going to sit here all day or what?'

'Hold on to your hats, folks,' Jake said. 'We're on our way!'

I laughed out loud again as the Volkswagen sailed down the drive and through the great steel gates that swung open silently to let us pass.

Jake turned right when we reached Sunset Boulevard and headed past the university towards the San Diego Freeway. There we joined the fast-moving stream of traffic heading south. We swung left onto the Santa Monica Freeway after a while and turned later onto the Santa Ana, and I marvelled yet again at the sheer size of the city, at the grey flat plain of buildings stretching into haze on either side of the freeway.

'I didn't expect LA to be so big,' I said to Jake, as I stared out at the downtown skyscrapers.

'Seventy square miles and three million people,' he said.

'I can believe it,' I said, peering at the line of gleaming chrome car bumpers ahead of us. 'And half of them heading for Disneyland, by the look of it.'

'This is the main freeway south to San Diego and Mexico,' Jake said. 'It's always busy.'

I turned and looked through the rear window at the traffic behind, and then I gasped. Immediately following us was a large black limousine with tinted windows. I couldn't see the driver's face clearly and I didn't know enough about American cars to tell if it was a Cadillac or not. But if it was . . .

Jake glanced at me curiously as I faced the front again. 'You okay?' he asked. 'You look as though you've seen a ghost or something.'

'I'm fine,' I said, trying to sound as casual as possible. 'Do you see that big car right behind us? It's a Chevrolet, isn't it?'

Jake glanced in his rear-view mirror. 'No, it's a Caddy. A Cadillac. Looks like a hearse, doesn't it?'

I didn't say anything. I stared stonily at the line of cars on the road ahead and told myself not to be so stupid. So what if it *was* a Cadillac? California was full of Cadillacs. It couldn't possibly be Jessica's. But she didn't approve of Jake. She hadn't liked the idea of us spending the day together. Perhaps she'd decided to have us followed. Perhaps it was Sam who was driving the car behind, watching every move we made . . .

'Are you *sure* you're feeling okay?' Jake said. 'We can go back home if you'd – '

'No,' I said quickly. 'Please, Jake, I'm fine. I'm just a bit tired, that's all. It's jet lag, I suppose.' Then I made a deliberate effort to forget about the car behind by smiling brightly at him and saying, 'Tell me about yourself. What were you doing on that plane anyway? I know hardly anything about you.'

'My parents live in London,' he said. 'They have done for a couple of years now. I'm a senior at the American School in London. I'm over here on vacation, but you know that already. What else can I tell you?'

'Everything,' I said. 'What's your favourite colour? What flavour ice cream do you like best? Which is your favourite band? Tell me everything!'

He laughed and started to tell me. But I didn't really hear what he said because I had turned back to look again at the car behind, at the black Cadillac which was still following us and which stayed with us all the way down the freeway to Anaheim.

Disneyland was as magical and exciting as I'd expected, and the few hours we spent there weren't nearly long enough to see all it had to offer. I added Disneyland to my mental list of places to revisit during my stay in California. I think I enjoyed Sleeping Beauty's Castle best but Jake's favourites were the Haunted House and the Mission to Mars space trip in 'Tomorrowland'.

The Big Thunder Mountain railroad was the most thrilling ride we tried and I remember screaming with delight as the runaway mine train whipped down the twisting mountain tracks. I remember, too, that Jake put an arm protectively round me and that I nestled comfortably against him. Suddenly nothing else seemed to matter and I forgot about Saxonwood and Jessica and the black Cadillac. Disneyland may have been a world of fantasy but I felt happier and safer there with Jake beside me than I did in the equally unbelievable world of Saxonwood.

At last the magical day came to an end and we headed north along the crowded freeways that had brought us to Disneyland that morning. This time no black limousine followed us, though I thought for one moment that I glimpsed it on the interchange with the Santa Monica Freeway. But there was no sign of it after that so I told myself that I was imagining things.

I felt my heart sink the closer we got to Saxonwood. I dreaded seeing Jessica and the others, and I didn't want to return to that beautiful, terrible house. I didn't want the day to end. I didn't want to leave Jake.

He was feeling the same way, I think, because he drove more and more slowly the closer we got to Bel Air and I thought the car would grind to a complete halt as we turned off Stone Canyon and headed up Stella Crest Drive. And then, suddenly, Jake swung the car to the side of the road and stopped.

'What's wrong?' I said. 'Have we run out of petrol or something?'

Jake turned and looked at me solemnly. 'No, we haven't run out of gas. I just don't want to say goodbye, that's all.'

I gave him a weak smile and hoped that he wouldn't notice that my hands were trembling. 'It's been a wonderful day,' I said. If I sat there long enough and he moved a little closer I'd be able to count every one of his freckles.

Jake put out his hand and ran a finger slowly down my

cheek. His touch was warm and gentle and, when I raised my face to his, he kissed me.

We didn't say anything for a while, not until he had kissed me again. And then he was the one who spoke first. 'Thanks for a great day,' he said huskily. 'How are you fixed for tomorrow?'

'I've nothing planned,' I said hesitantly, 'but I'm not – '

'It's okay,' he said. 'You don't have to see me again. You don't need to make excuses.'

'I'm not making excuses,' I said quickly. 'Oh, Jake, I'm not.' And I told him about the plans Jessica and Todd had made for me that day and how I felt that I ought to spend some time with them. After all, they were my hosts. I didn't tell Jake that I wanted to be with him more than anything else in the world. I didn't tell him that I didn't want to go back to Saxonwood. I didn't tell him that I felt frightened for no reason at all. Instead I said, 'Phone me tomorrow. I'll know then if they've made any plans.'

'Okay,' he said. 'I'll call you tomorrow. But I warn you, you haven't see the last of me yet, kid.'

'I'm glad to hear it,' I whispered. 'I'm really glad.'

Then he kissed me again, and then started the car and drove on, very slowly, to the gates of Saxonwood. It was only when we had turned into the drive that I glanced behind us and saw a black Cadillac following us towards the house.

Chapter Six

I leaped out of the Beetle the minute it drew to a halt outside Saxonwood and turned to look back at the Cadillac. The big limousine didn't follow us to the main entrance but took a side turning that led past the house to a garage block some distance away. There were rooms over the garage which I guessed were staff quarters. I couldn't see clearly who was driving the car because he was wearing a peaked cap that shaded his face, but I assumed it was Sam. But it could have been anyone. Todd, even. Anyone at all.

Jake was peering up at me curiously from the driving seat of his car. 'What's up?' he asked. 'Why are you so nervous, for Pete's sake?'

'Did you see that car?' I asked him urgently. 'The one that followed us up the drive?'

'I caught a glimpse of it,' he said. 'Why?'

'Do you think it's the one that was following us on the freeway this morning?'

Jake shrugged. 'I dunno. Could be. I didn't pay much attention to it – those limos all look the same to me.'

'I'm sure it was,' I said. 'I'm sure that – ' Then I stopped as I saw the mystified expression on his face. I gave a nervous laugh and said quickly, 'Oh, take no notice of me. I'm imagining things. Forget it.' I put out my hand to touch his. 'I'm just confused, I expect. Everything's so exciting and – and *different* here.'

'Some things are the same anywhere,' Jake said. 'Come here.' He pulled my face down to his and kissed me lightly on the lips. 'I'll call you tomorrow, okay?'

'Okay,' I whispered. I took a step back and he gave me a final wave before the garish little car chugged down the drive in the direction of the gates.

Then I turned round to go into the house and found myself staring straight at Jessica.

She was standing in the doorway of the house and, as I turned, I caught a look of intense anger in her dark eyes. Then her features relaxed into a broad smile and she stepped forward to meet me.

'Hi, Laura,' she said. 'Did you have a good day? Come in and have a soda or something.'

I followed Jessica into the dim hallway, hoping that she hadn't noticed my nervousness when I saw her. I wondered how much she had seen. How long had she been standing at the door, watching us? How much had she heard?

'I'll just go and freshen up.' I headed towards the stairs but I stopped when Jessica called me back.

I turned to face her and she came towards me, her hands outstretched. 'Laura, honey,' she said. 'Let's come to an agreement, shall we? I know that you're worried and confused by your father's will but don't let it spoil your stay with us. Let's just enjoy each other's company and let the lawyers and bankers and whoever sort out the business side of things. Okay? Is that a deal?' She took my hand in hers and squeezed it affectionately.

I stared at her for a moment, then I relaxed and smiled. 'It's a deal,' I said. 'I – I didn't know any of this was going to happen when – '

'Of course you didn't,' Jessica said soothingly. 'It's all been a great shock to you. To all of us. All the more reason why you should just relax and enjoy yourself. Let's leave the arguing to the professionals. It's what they're paid for.' She released my hand and smiled, and I wondered why I had been so wary of her. 'Hurry on down,' she said. 'We'll be out by the pool.'

As I showered and changed I remembered what Jessica had said and wondered yet again if I'd imagined her dislike of me. After all, what had I got to go on? I'd caught her giving me nasty looks but it was easy enough to misread people's expressions. And then there was the conversation I'd overheard. 'She's got to go. We've got to get rid of her.' There was no doubt about the words, I had heard them clearly enough. But there was no evidence that Jessica and Todd had been talking about *me*. They could have been talking about a maid. Anyone. Why should it be me? And then I remembered someone else talking, Dexter Shannon this time. 'If anything should happen to you, then your share of the estate and the house go to Jessica.' Wasn't that reason enough to get rid of me?

I stepped outside onto my balcony and stared down into the garden. Jessica and Verna were relaxing by the pool, cool drinks on a table by their side. Beyond them, the smooth lawns stretched into the distance, bathed in a constant spray of artificial rain from the hidden sprinklers. I couldn't believe that such a restful scene could hold any danger for me. It was impossible. And then I remembered Jessica by the oleander: 'Isn't it strange that something so beautiful can be so deadly?' And I shivered in the sunlight.

My fears faded into the back of my mind when I joined the others by the pool. Jessica asked me if I'd made plans for the next day and she seemed genuinely pleased when I said that I hadn't, that I thought it would be fun if the two of us could spend it together.

'Great idea,' she said. 'We'll do the town together. We could do some shopping, maybe, and then go out to a beach someplace. That is, if you'd like to.'

'I'd love it,' I said. 'I want to see *everything* in LA!'

By now Todd had joined us and he asked about my day. As I described our trip to Disneyland, I remembered the black Cadillac and anxiety seeped back into my mind. Where had Todd been all that day? And Jessica? If we *had* been followed by Jessica's car then no one else could have used it. Our trip to Disneyland had lasted at least six hours and no one at Saxonwood could have used the car during that time. Not if it had been following Jake's purple Beetle.

'And how have *you* spent the day?' I said brightly to the others. 'I bet none of you had as much fun as we did!'

'I guess you're right,' Verna said. 'I've been here all the time. This garden is so beautiful that some days I just hate to leave it. Jessica went out, though. Didn't you, dear?'

'Just to lunch with friends in Pacific Palisades,' Jessica smiled. 'Nothing very exciting about that.'

'Is that far?' I asked.

'Not really,' Jessica said.

'You're so lucky having Sam to drive you,' I said. 'I bet it takes no time at all to get round LA in the Cadillac.'

Jessica looked puzzled. 'I guess it does,' she said. 'But Sam didn't take me. I drove myself. I took the Porsche for a change. Anyway, the Caddy's been out of action all day. Sam took it off to be serviced this morning.'

I stared down into my glass. So the Cadillac had been out of action all day. Or had it? Maybe Sam had been following me instead.

'I'm more interested in how we're going to spend the *evening*,' Todd said then. 'How about it, cousin dear? Let's go down to Westwood after dinner and take in a movie. Unless,' he looked at me mockingly, 'you've something else planned. With Jake Shannon maybe?'

'I've nothing planned,' I said frostily.

I wasn't sure how to react to Todd's invitation. He seemed so distant and so sure of himself – I couldn't understand why he should want to spend an evening with me. I was so much younger than he was; surely he'd rather be with his own friends? Unless, of course, it was really Jessica's idea that he ask me out . . .

'Yes, I'd like to go to a movie,' I said. 'Thank you.'

Almost at once I wished I'd said no. I thought of my day with Jake and how he'd kissed me by the roadside and I felt a sharp pang of guilt. But it was too late to change my mind now. I had to go out with Todd, whether I liked it or not. I smiled to myself as I remembered how lonely I'd felt in London, and how I'd been convinced that no boy would ever show any interest in me. And now I was going out with *two* gorgeous men in the same day! It was hard to believe that all this was really happening to me. Things seemed to move so fast in California. Perhaps I really *was* in the middle of an exciting golden dream and any moment now I'd wake up and find myself back home in London.

After a leisurely dinner served as usual by the silent smiling maids, Todd and I left Jessica and Verna enjoying their coffee on the terrace and set off in his Peugeot. It wasn't far to Westwood Village, a district close to the university with streets crammed with cinemas, bookshops and restaurants of all kinds. We decided on a new Michael Douglas movie and afterwards we strolled along the crowded sidewalks for a while, enjoying impromptu performances by street musicians and mimes, and absorbing the exciting student atmosphere of the Village.

Todd was wonderful company. He seemed to go out of his way to be charming, and every time he looked at me with those clear blue eyes I felt my legs turn to jelly. I only hoped that I didn't look as goofy as I felt. I could tell that he didn't feel the same way about me; although he was attentive and friendly, he still seemed remote, and I felt more like his kid sister than his date. I wondered again why he was bothering to spend time with me instead of going out with his own friends. Was he simply being friendly to an English visitor or was there some other reason?

Before we left the house that evening I'd decided that I wouldn't respond to any questions about my father's will and my inheritance, but I needn't have worried – the subject didn't come up at all. I wondered if Todd had instructions from his mother to avoid talking about it. Perhaps she'd been serious when she told me that we should forget all about it and let the lawyers do the arguing for us. I hoped so. I really did hope so.

'Thank you for a lovely evening,' I said to Todd when we arrived back at Saxonwood.

He smiled at me as he closed the front door. 'The first of many, I hope,' he said lightly.

I didn't reply, and he went on, 'It's all right, there's no need to worry, cousin dear. I'm not going to make a nuisance of myself.' He shot me that familiar mocking glance. 'Not unless you want me to, that is.'

I laughed. 'You're forgetting that we're family. You're the one who keeps calling me "cousin dear", remember?'

'You know I'm only joking,' Todd said. The sharp blue eyes were serious now. 'You know as well as I do that we're not blood relations.'

I could feel my face reddening and I looked quickly away. But Todd reached out then and tilted my face towards his. He looked into my eyes for a moment or two and then kissed me lightly on the lips.

'Thanks for a great time, cousin dear,' he said with a laugh. 'See you tomorrow.' And he ran up the stairs, leaving me alone and speechless in the hall below.

Next morning, Jessica joined me downstairs for breakfast, much to my surprise. 'I thought I'd keep you company,' she said. 'Especially as we're going to be spending the whole day together.'

I smiled at her and glanced at the sunfilled gardens and the piercing blue sky. 'We're lucky,' I said. 'It looks as though it's going to be another beautiful day.'

It was only when Jessica stared at me as if I was out of my mind that I realised how stupid I must sound. *Every* day in California was beautiful; there was no need to be grateful for fine weather here.

Maria came outside then and told me that I was wanted on the phone. I wondered who on earth it could be at first and then I remembered. Of course. Jake.

'Hi,' he said. 'How've you been keeping?'

'Oh, fine.' I wondered whether to tell him about my trip to the movies with Todd and decided against it. I liked Jake a lot and didn't want to risk turning him away. 'I've missed you,' I said.

'Me too. Any chance of seeing you today?'

'I'm afraid not. Jessica's taking me shopping.'

'In the black Cadillac?' he asked.

Suddenly the morning turned cold. I'd forgotten all about the car. I think I'd convinced myself that all my fears had been imaginary. Now I wasn't so sure.

'I – I don't know,' I said. 'There seem to be lots of cars here.' Then, trying to be funny, 'Still, if we do go in the Cadillac, at least I'll know it won't be following us.' But even as I said this I knew that there was no need for me to be followed at all that day. Jessica would know exactly where I was.

'Can I see you tomorrow?' Jake asked. 'I'll pick you up at about the same time.'

'Okay,' I said.

'I wish it was tomorrow now,' he said huskily, and then, 'Bye, Laura,' before I had a chance to answer.

'Was that call from Jake Shannon?' Jessica asked when I returned to the breakfast table. 'He seems a pleasant young man. Ask him over for dinner some time.'

I gaped at her, unable to believe my ears. A couple of nights ago Jessica hadn't a good word to say about Jake, and now she was asking him to dinner. It didn't make sense. Perhaps I'd misjudged her, after all. Perhaps she was simply concerned about me spending time with a boy I hardly knew. Perhaps she was scared that Jake was only after my money, that he might marry me to get his hands on the inheritance. Perhaps she simply wanted to protect me from him. What if Jessica was right? What if Jake wasn't interested in *me* at all but only in my money? What if . . .

I told myself firmly not to be so stupid. It was much more likely that Jessica was worried in case I was after Jake, and not the other way round. Either way, if we got married, Saxonwood would slip further from her grasp than ever. She'd have to get rid of *both* of us. Soon.

Suddenly I got a fit of the giggles and nearly choked on my coffee. How crazy could I get? Perhaps I was suffering from sunstroke. Yes, that was it. Perhaps I had a touch of the sun. Perhaps that was why I was picturing Jessica as a mass-murderer. And as for Jake and I getting married – well, it was just ridiculous. I wasn't going to marry Jake or anyone. Not for years. Not yet, anyway.

'What's so funny?' Jessica's voice broke into my thoughts and I looked up to see her staring at me curiously.

'Oh, nothing,' I said quickly. 'Just – just a joke I remembered from the movie last night.'

She shrugged and said, 'I've asked Sam to bring the limo round at ten-thirty. Is that okay with you, Laura?'

I nodded. 'We're going in the Cadillac?'

'I think so. We won't have to waste time parking if Sam drives. It makes life a lot easier, believe me.'

My heart sank at the thought of Sam and the black limousine and then I told myself to snap out of it. I was going to enjoy myself today, come what may. I had nothing at all to worry about. Wicked stepmothers only existed in fairy tales and Jake wasn't after my money. I was on holiday in California and the sun was shining. What more could I ask?

We began the day by driving to the centre of the city where Jessica wanted me to see Olvera Street, the place where the first settlers in Los Angeles established a homestead. 'It's a tourist trap,' Jessica told me, 'but I think you'll find it interesting. And if you're looking for unusual gifts to take back home, there's no better place.'

She was right. Cobbled Olvera Street turned out to be a maze of shops and booths selling souvenirs and crafts of all kinds. Some of the buildings were old but most had been specially built to make the area look like an authentic Mexican village. We wandered around for some time, enjoying the performance of a strolling band, watching craftsmen at work on leather and silver, marvelling at the variety of crafts for sale. I even had my photograph taken astride a burro. I did buy one or two presents for the family – a colourful handpainted blanket called a serape, a decorated leather purse, a sombrero that I thought might make Jonathan laugh – but I was mainly content to enjoy the bustling Mexican atmosphere.

'Now for a complete contrast,' Jessica announced, as we set off in the Cadillac once again. 'Lunch at the Beverly Hills Hotel. Who knows, we may get to see some movie stars in the Polo Lounge.' She smiled at me. 'I must say it's fun being a tourist for a day.'

We had lunch in the elegant Coterie restaurant overlooking the pool at the Beverly Hills Hotel, an enormous pink building surrounded by acres of tropical gardens. Jessica told me that the hotel was a celebrated meeting place for movie stars, some of whom rented bungalows in the grounds, but I didn't notice any – well, none that I recognised, anyway. Everyone there *looked* like movie stars, though, whether they were or not, and I felt distinctly shabby and out-of-place among so many beautiful people. I whispered as much to Jessica as we were ushered to our table but she looked at me in surprise and said, 'But Laura dear, you look so fresh and charming. I'm sure the rest of us must seem terribly old and raddled in comparison. Now then, I can recommend the scallop mousse. And the veal with apple brandy is out of this world.'

I could hardly move after the meal and all I wanted to do was go to sleep but Jessica only laughed when I suggested we spend the afternoon by the pool at Saxonwood. 'What nonsense you do talk, Laura,' she said. 'We've only just started our day.'

Jessica's energy seemed inexhaustible. 'Main Street, Santa Monica,' she snapped at Sam when the Cadillac drew up beside us outside the restaurant. 'You'll love Santa Monica,' she said to me. 'The beach is famous, of course, but I want you to see Main Street. It's a shopping area built to look like a street in an old Western town.'

I smiled brightly at her but my heart sank. I'd seen enough shops and galleries and souvenir stalls to last a lifetime. But I had to agree that Main Street was attractive, and I found some Navajo beadwork in a craft shop there that would make an ideal gift for Abby. After that, Sam drove us down to the beach, and I gasped with delight at the miles of sand and at the blue-green Pacific stretching forever. Sam dropped us off at the pier, and Jessica and I strolled along it, enjoying the brisk sea air and the old-fashioned amusement arcades, marvelling at the enormous old merry-go-round – or carousel, as Jessica called it. By now, even she had begun to wilt and so, when we returned to the car, she told Sam to head back home. This time I couldn't wait to get back to the peace of Saxonwood and the cool inviting water of the swimming pool.

'That was a wonderful trip,' I said to Jessica as the Cadillac purred up the drive at last. 'Thank you so much.'

'I've enjoyed it too,' she smiled. 'You're good company, Laura. Now I'm going to collapse on my bed for an hour, I think. How about you?'

'A swim,' I said, thinking longingly of the pool. 'A very long swim, and a long iced drink. Though I'm not sure in which order.'

As I lay in the sun by the pool, drying off after my swim, I thought about the day and how different everything seemed now. Jessica had been charming and friendly, with no trace of the hostility I'd sensed when I first arrived at Saxonwood. Surely I'd only imagined her coolness. I'd been so tired and confused when I arrived that I hadn't been thinking straight. I couldn't believe now that Jessica wanted to harm me. I'd misunderstood the conversation I'd overheard, and only imagined that the Cadillac had been following me. I knew that now.

That evening Todd announced at dinner that he was going with some friends to a jazz club in Redondo Beach. I looked down at my plate when he said this, hoping against hope that he'd ask me to go with him. But he didn't, of course. I told myself firmly that it didn't really matter, and that an early night would do me good after my tiring day's sightseeing with Jessica. But secretly I was bitterly disappointed. I'd have given anything for another evening out with Todd. It didn't matter that he wasn't really interested in me; it would have been enough just to be with him. Then I told myself not to be so stupid. Todd was much too old for me and anyway, I couldn't stand jazz.

Next morning I was ready and waiting on the front steps when Jake's purple Volkswagen came stuttering up the drive. My heart leaped when I saw his cheerful freckled face grinning up at me from the driver's seat, and I laughed out loud with delight when he called out to me, 'Your carriage awaits, ma'am.'

'It wasn't as funny as all that,' he said when I climbed into the car beside him.

'No, it wasn't,' I said. 'I'm just so pleased to see you, that's all.'

He beamed at me. 'Are you? Are you really?' And he kissed me, very slowly.

'Where are we going today?' I asked, as I pushed him away at last. I didn't want the kissing to stop but I had a feeling that someone was watching us from the house.

'Anywhere you like,' he said. 'Katmandu? Babylon? Bulgaria?'

'Idiot!' I said. 'No, seriously, where?'

'I thought maybe up to Mulholland Drive and down to Universal City for a tour of the movie studios. And then on to a beach someplace. Las Tunas, maybe, or Topanga.'

'Sounds okay to me,' I said. 'Let's go.'

We turned left when we came to Sunset Boulevard and then left again up Beverly Glen, heading towards the indigo mountains that rose ahead of us to meet the brilliant sky. As we drove, the road began to twist and turn as it ran into a shadowy canyon. Houses hugged the road on each side and rocky hillsides rose steeply behind them, covered in scrub and creepers.

For some reason that I couldn't explain I began to feel nervous. I kept remembering my last trip with Jake and how we were followed by the black Cadillac. Every now and then I glanced through the rear window, fully expecting to see the menacing black and chrome bulk on the road behind. I was aware of Jake looking at me curiously whenever I did this, and I hoped he wouldn't ask me what the matter was.

We rounded a curve and suddenly the houses stopped and the steep banks on either side were no longer green from constant watering but dry and rocky. Long brittle grass and grey weeds sprouted by the road and the mountainside was thick with sagebrush and thorn trees. On and up we climbed and then, at last, we reached the crest of the mountains and turned off along a twisting narrow road. After a while we came to a look-out point high on the ridge, and Jake pulled in and stopped.

I climbed gratefully out of the car, and then gasped when I saw the view. On one side, I could see Los Angeles spreading away as far as the eye could see. And then, on the other side of the ridge, another sea of houses disappearing into haze.

'San Fernando Valley,' Jake said. 'On a clear day you can see as far as the Sierra Madre from here. And down the coast to Balboa.'

'There's so much of it,' I said weakly. 'I thought that LA ended at these mountains.'

We stood in silence for a while, and then Jake put his arm around me and kissed me gently on the cheek. 'You seemed nervous on the way up here,' he said, and then, in a Bugs Bunny voice, 'What's up, Doc?'

I hesitated, wondering whether to tell him the truth or not. And then, seeing the concern in his eyes, I decided to take the plunge. I told Jake everything. I told him about the will and my inheritance, and about my fears about Jessica and Todd. I told him about the conversation I'd overheard at Saxonwood and the black Cadillac that had followed us to Disneyland. I even told him that I was scared that *he* was after me for my money.

There was a long pause when I finished, and then Jake put both arms tightly round me and kissed me. I felt suddenly secure and safe.

'You're a nut,' he whispered. 'An adorable nut.'

'You don't think I'm going mad?' I said anxiously, running my finger gently down his cheek.

'No,' he smiled. 'Of course not. But I think maybe you've got things a bit haywire. I can't believe that Jessica Cordell would harm you – or anyone else for that matter. And she's a very rich woman. She doesn't need your money, believe me.'

'So you think I'm imagining it all?'

He looked at me for a moment and then nodded slowly. 'Yes,' he said. 'I do.'

It was as if a shadow had passed over the sun. Suddenly the day didn't seem as warm as it had before, and the world didn't seem as bright.

'Come on,' I said abruptly. 'Let's get going. *If* we're going.'

We got back into the car in silence, and Jake steered it back onto the narrow road. Neither of us said anything for a while; I stared stonily ahead at the barren mountainside dropping steeply away on our left.

'I'm sorry, Laura,' Jake said at last. 'You asked my opinion and I gave it to you. I just can't believe that someone like Jessica would try to harm you.'

'That's okay,' I said stiffly. 'Don't worry about it.'

We rounded a corner and the road narrowed even

more. On our right, barren rock towered to the sky and, on the left, the ground fell away in a mass of scattered stone and scrub.

And then I saw it. The Cadillac. The familiar chrome and black shape was coming towards us, driving very fast on the narrow road. I remember shouting, 'There it is! The car!' and then Jake's breathless, 'Jeepers! It's coming straight for us!'

He sounded his horn but the driver of the Cadillac didn't seem to hear. The car continued to drive straight towards us, on the wrong side of the road.

'Get out of the way!' Jake yelled but it didn't make any difference. The black car came relentlessly on. I caught a brief glimpse of the driver's eyes, dark beneath a peaked cap, before Jake desperately swung the Beetle out of the path of the limousine, and we skidded off the road and down the bank, coming to rest at last against a drift of tumbled rock.

Chapter Seven

Everything was a blur after that. I remember Jake shouting at me, asking if I was all right, and I remember wondering whether I was dead or not and deciding that I wasn't because my arm was hurting too much. And then I remember Jake helping me out of the car and how surprised we both were to see that the Beetle looked okay, apart from a large dent on one side and a few scratches. And then he put his arms around me and we clung to each other for a while, trying to get over the shock. We'd been lucky. If we'd left the road a little further on, the car would have tumbled into a steep canyon. Fortunately the slope here was more gentle and little damage had been done to the car or to ourselves.

I'm not sure what happened then. I think we began to scramble up the hillside to the road. I remember how hot it was, and how dry and dusty everything seemed under that brilliant sky. We reached the road at last and stopped for a moment, uncertain what to do next. I remember very clearly that Jake turned to me and grinned ruefully, and that I reached out to brush a streak of dust from his face.

'My aunt's going to kill me after this,' he said. 'She'll never let me drive her car again.'

I remember feeling cross then and saying sharply, 'Just be glad that the *Caddy* didn't kill you.'

Jake nodded and then said slowly, 'That guy really did try to kill us. I can't believe it, it's so – '

'At least you know I was telling the truth,' I said. 'Now you've got to believe that I was right about the car following us and someone wanting to harm me.'

'I have to,' he said. 'Unless the crash was an accident.'

'An accident? You're joking! How could it be? He came straight towards us, he forced us off the road – '

'I know, I know,' Jake said wearily. 'It was no accident. It was deliberate. I just can't believe it happened, that's all.'

'Well, it did!' I snapped. 'Jessica's trying to kill me!'

'She wasn't driving that car. It was a man.'

'I know that,' I said impatiently. 'It was Sam, her driver. I'm sure of that now. She got him to do it.'

Jake stared at me and suddenly burst out laughing. 'Oh no!' he said. 'That's going too far, Laura. It wasn't Sam or Jessica. It was just some nut, that's all. Some freak out to harm us for no reason at all.'

I think I stalked angrily away from him then, and he followed me down the road a short way. Soon after that, as if in answer to a prayer, a highway patrol car appeared from nowhere and screeched to a halt in a cloud of dust. I have confused memories then of lots of talking, and driving very fast down twisting roads, and then the dim hall at Saxonwood and someone helping me up the stairs – Verna, I think, or Maria – and then the cool peace of my room and the welcome comfort of my bed. And then sleep. Sleep.

But I didn't sleep for long. I woke up from a confused dream about a gigantic Cadillac with vicious fangs to find myself shaking uncontrollably. And then, almost at once, the door opened and Verna came into the room. She crossed to the bed and looked down at me anxiously.

'Laura, dear,' she said. 'The doctor's here. He's coming up now, okay?'

I sat up in bed and said, 'Doctor? I don't need a doctor. I'm okay. I'm – '

'Now then, of course you do,' Verna said soothingly, and pushed me back onto the pillow. 'You've had an accident. You're shocked and you say your arm hurts. Of course you must see a doctor.' She wandered over to the window and looked out into the garden, a worried expression on her face. 'If only I could get hold of Jessica, she'd know how to handle this. But she's out all day – '

'*No!*' I screamed, and Verna turned round in surprise. 'No, please,' I repeated, more quietly this time. 'I don't want to see her. She's the one who . . .' My voice tailed away then. Could I trust Verna? Could I trust any of them?

Verna came back to the bedside and said urgently, 'What do you mean, Laura? Jessica's the one who did what?'

I stared miserably up at her and shook my head. I closed my eyes, hoping that she wouldn't ask me any more. Fortunately the doctor arrived then and Verna left the room. He was middle-aged and gentle, and he said that there were no bones broken but there was some bruising. He also said I was in shock and should stay in bed for the next couple of days. After that he told me how pleased he was to meet me again but he wished it could have been some other way. He'd been my father's doctor for years, and remembered me as a baby. After a while he went away, saying he would leave some medication with Verna, and a little later she appeared once again, with a tray of juice and water and a couple of pills that I had to take right away.

The next thing I remember was waking up to find Jessica standing by my bed. At first I thought I was dreaming again and that she was part of a nightmare, but when she spoke I knew I was awake.

'Laura, darling,' she said. 'I'm so shocked to hear what happened. How are you feeling now?'

'I'm okay,' I mumbled. 'I'll be fine, really. We ran off the road, that's all.'

'That's all!' Jessica sounded indignant. If I hadn't known better I would have thought she really cared. 'That's all? You might have been killed!'

And aren't you disappointed that I wasn't, I thought grimly to myself.

Jessica sat down on a chair by the bed. 'I knew something like this would happen,' she said. 'I knew Jake Shannon wasn't to be trusted. I knew he was a no-good – '

'It wasn't Jake's fault!' I shouted. 'The other car came straight for us. Jake saved my life. There's nothing wrong with him, he's – '

'Now, don't upset yourself,' Jessica said quickly. 'The doctor said you need peace and rest. But I don't care what you say, Laura. If you hadn't been out with Jake Shannon then none of this would have happened. And he had the nerve to call the house just now. I soon told him – '

'Jake phoned? Why didn't you tell me? Why didn't you let me speak to him?'

'Because you were resting,' Jessica said wearily. 'You were asleep. I told him you were fine and he said he'd call back later. Okay?'

I nodded feebly, and Jessica stood up. 'Now I'm going to leave you to get some more rest. Maria will be up soon with a little dinner. An omelette, maybe, nothing fancy.'

'Thank you,' I said, and turned my face away.

Jessica stood by my bed for a moment in silence, and then I heard her quietly leave the room.

This time I didn't sleep. I felt frightened. And so alone. I wanted to talk to Jake. Suddenly this seemed the most important thing in the world. I felt safe with him. He'd know what to do, he'd know how to help me. And then I remembered his impatient voice saying, 'I can't believe that Jessica would try to harm you.' He didn't believe me. But he *did* care for me, and I knew that he'd help me.

When Maria brought my dinner I asked her where the nearest phone was. She laughed, and said that I *must* be feeling ill. Hadn't I noticed that there was a phone in my room, on a low table by the armchair? I smiled and said that I'd forgotten, and she brought it over to me and put it down on the bedside cabinet. I decided to make the call as soon as she'd left the room – the rest of the family would be at dinner and no one would interrupt me.

It was Ethel Shannon who answered. She seemed

surprised to hear from me but was anxious to know how I was feeling.

'Oh, I'm so glad,' she said when I told her I was fine. 'I know Jake would love to speak with you but he's out with his uncle tonight, visiting friends in Glendale. I'll tell him to call you tomorrow.'

I felt a surge of panic as I put down the receiver. There was no one I could turn to, no one at all. I was on my own. If only I'd never come to California. Everything would have been all right if I'd stayed at home with Maxine and Jonathan and Abby. Abby. Abby's father lived in Los Angeles and she'd given me his number before I left home. Perhaps he would help me, perhaps he'd believe I was telling the truth.

With growing excitement I burrowed in my bedside table for the notebook where I'd written Billy Day's phone number. He was an important movie star but I'd met him several times when he'd visited us in London and I knew he'd remember me. Wouldn't he?

I found the number and dialled. And then my heart sank as the call went through to an answering service. Mr Day was out of town for a few days but if I cared to leave my name and number . . . I told the friendly operator that, no, I wouldn't leave my name, I'd call back next week, thank you very much.

'You're welcome,' she said. 'Have a nice day now.'

Have a nice day. That was a laugh. Anyway, it wasn't even daytime any more. And how was I supposed to have a nice day when –

And then I realised what I'd heard. A click on the line. I'd kept the receiver to my ear for a moment after the operator had hung up, and I'd heard a click on the line. Someone had been listening. Someone had been listening on an extension. Someone in the house.

I didn't eat my omelette. And I refused to touch the fruit that Maria brought in to me later. I couldn't stop shaking and my mouth was dry with fear. I drank some coffee after a while and took the pills that Verna brought me when she came up to bed. Jessica came in for a moment to say goodnight, and Todd popped his head round the door, and then I was left on my own to drift in and out of sleep once more. And I dreamed again of a huge car with a radiator grille like grinning teeth that chased me down a long twisting canyon . . .

I awoke with a start, knowing that I had heard a noise. A sharp sudden noise on the balcony. I sat up in bed and stared into the darkness, my heart pounding like a sledgehammer. There was someone out there. I knew it. There was someone on the balcony.

The room was very dark with only a glimmer of light seeping through the curtains. Perhaps I'd been dreaming again. But then I heard the noise once more, a distinct scuffing sound as if someone was dragging their feet on the balcony. And then I heard something else, the creak of the handle on the French windows.

There was someone out there. There was someone on the balcony. Someone was trying to come in.

Chapter Eight

I think I screamed then. In fact, I must have done for, after a moment or two, I heard running footsteps and then my bedroom door was flung open and the light was switched on. Todd was standing in the doorway, his blue eyes wide with concern. 'Laura, what's the matter?' he asked urgently.

A wave of terror swamped me again and I pointed at the windows and gasped, 'Out there! There's someone on the balcony, trying to get in!'

I sank back on the pillows and closed my eyes, wishing that I could stop shaking. And then I heard the windows opening and Todd's footsteps on the balcony. Then I heard him come back into the room and the sound of the windows being gently closed, and I opened my eyes again, dreading what I might see.

By now Jessica had appeared in the doorway, wearing some sort of filmy negligée. 'What's happened?' she said urgently. 'I heard someone scream. What's going on?'

I stared at Todd. 'Who – who was there?' I stammered. 'Did you catch him? Did you – '

He stood by the bed for a moment, looking down at me. There was a worried look on his face.

'Well?' Jessica demanded. 'Isn't anyone going to tell me what's going on around here?'

Todd turned to her. 'Laura thought she heard

someone outside on the balcony. I've checked but there's no one there. They must have got away or else . . .' His voice tailed away into silence.

I stared at him open-mouthed. He didn't believe me. I could tell that he didn't believe me. 'There was someone there,' I shouted. 'There *was* someone there. I heard him – '

'Him?' Jessica said quickly. 'How did you know it was a man?'

'Well – I – I don't know,' I stammered. 'I just assumed it must be – I don't know . . .'

'I guess you were having a bad dream,' Todd said quietly. 'You're still shocked from the accident.'

'I *did* hear something,' I said dully. 'I *did*. I *know* I did.'

I closed my eyes again, not wanting to see the puzzled concern on Todd's face. Or the suspicion on Jessica's.

'What's going on? What's all the noise about?'

I opened my eyes to see Verna running into the room. She was dressed in an elegant ivory housecoat, and her face looked old and strained without its make-up.

'Laura's had a bad dream,' Jessica said impatiently. 'She had a nightmare and screamed, that's all.'

'I heard someone on the balcony,' I said defiantly. I didn't feel frightened any more, just angry. I was angry with myself for reacting so hysterically to the noise. I should have kept quiet and got out of bed to investigate. And I was angry at Todd and Jessica because they didn't believe me. How dared they accuse me of imagining it? Unless – unless that was what they *wanted* me to think. Maybe they had planned it themselves. Maybe they were deliberately trying to frighten me, first with the accident, and now with an intruder on the balcony. Maybe it was a plot. They were trying to frighten me, frighten me away. But why? Why?

'Oh, you poor dear!' Verna said, and she pushed past Jessica and came and sat down on the bed. 'Of *course* you had a bad dream. You've been in an accident and you're still in shock.' She took my hand in hers and smiled at me. 'What you need is peace and quiet, well away from Saxonwood. You need to be someplace where you can relax and recover without being disturbed, where you can forget all about the accident and get back to normal.'

I nodded. That was exactly what I needed. 'I – I think I'd like to go home,' I said. 'Back to London. As soon as possible.'

'Don't be silly now,' Verna said, patting my hand. 'You can't do that. Why, you're not fit to travel, for one thing. Doctor Aronson prescribed peace and quiet for the next few days. And anyway, you've only just arrived. You don't want to go flying off before we've had a chance to get to know you, now do you?'

I didn't say that I wanted that more than anything else in the world. I didn't say that I *did* want to go flying off, back to London and home. But Verna was right. I wasn't well enough to travel. And then there was Jake . . .

Verna leaned towards me conspiratorially. 'I've got a nice little place up at Malibu,' she whispered. 'It's right on the beach and so peaceful, you wouldn't believe it.

There's nothing to do there but swim and watch the surf. You'd love it. Now what I suggest – '

Jessica said quickly, 'Now, Verna, I don't think that Laura should leave Saxonwood just yet. She needs attention and good food. I'm sure Doctor Aronson wouldn't approve.' She exchanged a worried glance with Todd who chimed in, 'I think she *should* stay with us, Verna. We can look after her better here.'

Verna shot them a withering glance. 'What the child needs is peace and quiet without you all fussing over her. We can cook for ourselves quite easily, or else take Maria or one of the others with us. And Malibu isn't the end of the world. We can get to the doctor if we need to, and he can get to us.' She turned back to me. 'How about it, Laura? How do you feel about spending a couple of days at the beach with your old American aunt?'

I smiled at her gratefully. 'I'd like it. Thank you.'

'Good.' Verna stood up and headed for the door. 'I'll send someone to open up the house tomorrow and then we can move in the day after maybe, if you're feeling well enough.'

'Oh, I'll be well enough,' I said. 'Just you try and stop me.'

'I still think it's a crazy idea,' Jessica said. 'You can have peace and quiet *here*, Laura. As much as you want.'

I remembered the man on the balcony and the Cadillac heading straight towards me on that narrow road, and I shook my head. 'I think the change will do me good,' I said. 'It'll be great to be by the sea.'

'I'll call Doctor Aronson tomorrow,' Jessica said coldly. 'We'll see what *he* thinks.' She looked at Todd. 'Well, I guess we'd all better leave you in peace now. You could do with some sleep. And so could the rest of us. Goodnight, Laura.'

When they had all gone, I lay awake for a while, alert for the slightest sound outside, for any suggestion of an intruder in the house or grounds. Then the next thing I knew was a tap on the door and Maria coming into my room with coffee and fruit juice. It was morning, and the room was bathed in sunlight.

I stayed in my room that morning but I began to grow restless towards lunchtime and so I got out of bed, took a leisurely shower, and made my way downstairs. I was still feeling a bit shaky so I settled down in a lounger on the terrace to enjoy the sun for a while. As I looked across the brilliant gardens, I realised that I could never feel at ease at Saxonwood, despite the comfort of the house and the splendour of the grounds. Now, I couldn't wait to leave them. I longed for tomorrow, when Verna and I would set off for her house at Malibu. I had a vision of a long sandy beach edged with tumbling surf, and I wished that we were there now, far away from the sinister cloying beauty of Saxonwood.

Both Verna and Jessica were at home for lunch and we ate a light seafood salad followed by orange sorbet at a table by the pool. Verna talked non-stop throughout the meal about the Malibu house and what a marvellous time we were going to enjoy there. She'd spoken to Doctor Aronson that morning and he'd said that he had nothing against the idea, provided that I took things easy. Verna had promised him that she'd see to that.

'I still think it would be best if you stayed here,' Jessica said. 'We can look after you better at Saxonwood, Laura, believe me.'

But I shook my head. I had to get away from her and from the house. I no longer felt safe there. And I needed time to think, to sort out my feelings for Jake and about Jessica and Todd. If my fears were mistaken, and if I *was* imagining all that had happened, then maybe a few quiet days by the sea would help me to get things into perspective. No, come what may, I *had* to get away. And as soon as possible.

Afterwards, Verna and Jessica left me in the shade by the pool and I dozed for a while, enjoying the peace of the gardens. I must have dropped off to sleep, I think, because I remember waking up with a start to find Jake looking down on me, a cheerful grin on his face.

'Hi!' he said. 'You look beautiful when you're asleep.'

'Only then?' I teased.

'No, not only then. All the time.' He sat down beside me and then leaned over and kissed me. 'How are you feeling?' he said after a while, and then kissed me slowly again before I was able to reply.

'I feel fine,' I said at last. 'Especially now that you're here.'

'I got a very frosty reception from Mrs Cordell,' he said ruefully. 'That lady sure doesn't like me for some reason.'

I quickly changed the subject. 'How's the car? Is it badly damaged?'

'No, not too badly. But Aunt Ethel's pretty mad about what happened. She says it's the last time I'll ever drive any car of hers.'

'Oh, she'll change her mind,' I said, then, 'Did you tell the police everything that happened?'

'Sure I did,' he said, looking away. 'But they've only our word for it. We've no evidence. Unless *you* happened to note the licence plate of the Caddy?'

I shook my head.

'Well, then,' Jake said. 'They haven't got very much to go on, have they? Not unless that guy tries the same trick again.'

'Well, he'd better hurry up because I'm not going to be here much longer,' I said.

Jake looked puzzled and so I said that I was going to Malibu with Verna the next day. And then, because he asked why, I told him everything that had happened the night before. When I had finished, he kissed me gently on the cheek and said, 'You poor kid. I guess that accident shook you up pretty badly.'

I stared at him. 'What do you mean?'

He looked surprised and said, 'Well, you must have been upset to imagine the noises. I mean, there wasn't really anyone on the balcony, was there? You only *thought* you heard someone.'

I couldn't believe my ears. He didn't believe me either. Jake was just like the others, like Verna and Jessica and Todd. He didn't believe me. No one believed me.

'I expect you're right,' I said, and gave him a weak smile.

'Malibu's a great place,' Jake said cheerfully. 'Maybe I'll come up and see you. What's the address?'

'I don't know,' I said listlessly.

I wasn't sure if I wanted to see Jake again, not if he didn't believe me. He had been my last hope. But I couldn't trust him now. I couldn't trust anyone. I had no one to turn to. No one at all. I was on my own.

Chapter Nine

Verna's beach house wasn't at all what I expected. For some reason I'd pictured it as being small and uncomfortable, rather like the holiday cottage in Cornwall that Maxine had rented a couple of summers before. But Verna's house couldn't have been more different. For one thing, it was huge, with at least five bedrooms and an enormous living room with floor-to-ceiling windows. And for another, it was a proper house, with luxurious furniture and everything else necessary for comfortable California living. But it was the setting that really took my breath away. The house was built right on the beach. There was a wide verandah running all the way along the front – Verna called it 'the deck' and it did feel at times as though one was on a ship – and steps led straight down from there to the gleaming white sand below which stretched into the distance on either side. Behind the house, there was a garden which seemed to be carved out of the rocky cliffs that plunged steeply to the shore.

As we drove north to Malibu along the Pacific Coast Highway, Verna had told me that she'd lived there all the year round when she was married. 'But I always longed to get back to Saxonwood,' she said. 'So when – when the marriage ended, I went back home. It was where I belonged.'

'And your husband?' I asked. 'Did he – '

'Oh, he died,' Verna said lightly. 'He was drowned.' She shot me a bright nervous smile and the Plymouth swerved alarmingly. 'He drowned right outside the house, as a matter of fact.'

I gave a nervous laugh. 'Well, I'm not surprised you couldn't carry on living there.'

'I did think of selling the place,' Verna said dreamily. 'But it's a lovely house and it comes in useful for vacations and weekends. The sea is so beautiful. I could sit and look at it all day.'

Verna was right. The sea *was* beautiful, but it was wild at times too and I spent hours on those first few days just sitting on the deck, watching the waves smash on the shining sand. The house lay to the north of Malibu and so there weren't many other houses nearby; at times it seemed as though the entire beach and the great blue-green Pacific Ocean itself were our private property. I'll always remember that magical setting: the white sand, hot between my bare toes when I ran down to the sea in the morning; the surf foaming around the rocks that had tumbled into the ocean from a landslide the winter before; gulls wheeling over the glittering water; and, on the distant horizon, wisps of smoke from passing freighters.

We didn't do much during the day – I slept and swam and sunbathed, hoping for the California tan that Jessica had promised me, and Verna sat on the deck and read or pottered in the kitchen. We had decided to look after ourselves, and Verna had volunteered to do the cooking. One afternoon we drove in the Plymouth to the nearby J. Paul Getty Museum, built to look like a Roman villa and filled with an astonishing collection of paintings, sculpture and antiquities. Rembrandt, Rubens and Gainsborough seemed strangely out of place under the blazing sun of Malibu but California was full of such surprises. Occasionally we went out for drives along the coast but mostly we just stayed at the house, enjoying the peace. In the evenings we talked, and watched television, or looked through Verna's scrapbooks. The Malibu house was where she kept the photographs and scripts and other souvenirs of her acting career, and she would often reminisce about her Hollywood days as we sat on the deck in the evenings, looking out across the dark pounding surf.

As day followed golden day, I began to relax and feel rested. Soon Saxonwood seemed little more than a bad dream. Jessica phoned every day to find out how I was, and Todd came on the line too if he was at home. They didn't come to see us, though, and I was glad about that. I didn't want to be reminded of all that had happened. But, as the days passed, I began to wonder whether Jake and the others hadn't been right, after all. Perhaps I *had* imagined the intruder on the balcony and the car following us to Disneyland. Perhaps the accident with the Beetle had been exactly that, an accident, and surely I'd simply misheard Jessica's threat on that very first afternoon.

I didn't hear from Jake, of course, but then I didn't expect to. He had no idea where I was, and I didn't want to speak to him until I'd sorted out my feelings for him. I missed him, though. I longed for him to be there with me, to share the long lazy days on the empty beach, and the calm moonlit evenings. I think it was then that I realised that I was in love with Jake and that I wanted to be with him always. But how could I be sure of his feelings for me? He didn't believe that someone had been following us or that there had been a man on my balcony. If he didn't trust me, then how could he love me? And how could I love him?

It was on the morning of our fifth day at Malibu that I woke up knowing that I'd had enough and that I wanted to go back to Saxonwood. The past four days had been wonderful but I realised now that the time had come to take up my life where I had left off. I'd recovered from the shock of the accident and I had no excuse for staying away any longer. Besides, I was beginning to feel restless. Days of sun and swimming were all very well but I still had so much to see and do in California. And I knew that I wanted to see Jake. More than anything else I wanted to see Jake.

As we sat on the deck, enjoying our breakfast in the morning sun, I told Verna that I'd like to go back to Los Angeles as soon as possible.

She stared at me for a moment, her eyes wide with surprise. 'Surely not,' she said at last. 'We're having *such* a wonderful time here. I thought you liked it. I thought – '

'Oh, I *do*!' I said quickly, putting my hand over hers. 'I love it here. It's wonderful. It's – oh, it's one of the loveliest places I've ever seen. But I can't stay here any longer. There's so much I still want to see and do before

I go back to England. And Jessica will think I'm awfully rude if I stay away much longer.'

'Well, I'll think about it.' Verna's eyes were hard and cold, and I was taken aback by the harshness of her voice. 'I'll think about it. I'm not sure if *I* want to go back yet. I'm not sure at all.'

'Well, there's no need for you to leave too,' I said brightly. 'You could stay on here, couldn't you?'

'Stay here alone? I wouldn't be safe.' She shook her head. 'No, I don't want to go yet. Maybe in a day or two. Maybe I'll feel differently then.'

I shrugged, and changed the subject. Perhaps she was right. Another couple of days wouldn't do any harm and besides, I still had some work to do on my tan. A few more hours in the sun would work wonders. They wouldn't recognise me next term at Chalfont.

It wasn't until the next day that I raised the subject again but Verna hadn't changed her mind. This time she adopted a pleading tone. 'Surely you don't want to leave here so soon? Please, for my sake, just a day or two more?'

I smiled and nodded, but I no longer felt happy about staying on. Suddenly the beautiful house was beginning to seem like a prison. Verna suggested that we take a trip to see an old Spanish mission near Ventura that day but I said no. I was in no mood for enjoying myself.

'Look, dear,' she said that evening, after we'd eaten a silent dinner, 'we'll go back soon, I promise. Maybe tomorrow, or the next day.' I looked up at her hopefully and she went on dreamily, 'Mind you, I don't blame you for wanting to go back to Saxonwood. It's so beautiful, isn't it? I've always loved the house, ever since I can remember. We grew up there, your father and I.'

I nodded. 'I know. You've already told me.'

She looked at me vaguely. 'Have I? Yes, I guess I have. Your grandfather built the house, you know, as a wedding present for my mother. I was born there. And your father too. I do love it so. And I know that *you'll* grow to love it too when you come over here to live.'

I looked at Verna in surprise. 'But I'm not going to live over here.' I gave a nervous laugh. 'I couldn't. My home's in London. And anyway, I could never live at Saxonwood. It's – it's just too *big*. What would I do with a house that size? Oh no, I could never live *there*. Never.'

There was a pause, and then, 'I'm sorry to hear that,' Verna said at last. 'Very sorry indeed.' Her voice seemed suddenly harsh. 'You know, Laura, I couldn't bear the thought of anything happening to Saxonwood. If it fell into the wrong hands, I'd – ' She didn't finish the sentence but she didn't really need to. I could tell from the look of fierce anger on her face exactly what she had in mind. It was then that I remembered my father's will and that I was now the owner of Saxonwood. Until now, it hadn't meant much to me, it had been just one of the many unreal things that had happened to me since I arrived in California. Now, hearing Verna talk about the house and seeing how much she cared about it, I felt suddenly uneasy. I knew that I had to leave Malibu as soon as possible.

I cleared my throat nervously and said, 'I think I'd

better go back tomorrow, if you don't mind. I've had a lovely time here but I must – '

'I don't want to go,' Verna said coldly. 'I don't want to go yet. Not yet.'

'Maybe not,' I said, hoping that I didn't sound as anxious as I felt. 'But *I* want to go. I *must* go. If you won't drive me then I'll ask Todd to come and fetch me. Or I'll order a cab. I'm sorry but I really must go back tomorrow.'

Verna said nothing. She was staring into space, her face expressionless.

'I – I think I'll go and pack now.' I got to my feet and went inside to my room, leaving her sitting at the table in silence.

I woke up late the next morning and when I came out of my room I found Verna sitting motionless on the deck, staring out to sea. I shouted a quick, 'Good morning!' to her as I ran down to the beach for my regular morning swim, and when I returned to the house twenty minutes later I was surprised to see that she was still there, looking as though she hadn't moved at all.

She gave me a vague smile when I joined her on the deck. I smiled back and said, 'Look, I really must get back to Saxonwood today. I'd be very grateful if you'd drive me there. I'm all packed so any time will do.'

Verna gave me a pitying smile. 'Drive you? Oh, I can't do that, dear. Anyway, the car's not working. I can't get it started.'

I stared at her in silence. 'What's wrong with it?' I said at last.

Verna shrugged. 'I wouldn't know. Everything under

that hood's a mystery to me. I guess you'll just have to put up with this place a little while longer.'

I didn't know what to say. Verna was lying, of course. The car had been working perfectly the day before when we'd gone into Malibu for groceries. I couldn't believe that the engine had failed for no reason at all. She was lying. She was trying to keep me from leaving. Well, I'd soor put a stop to that.

I stood up and said, 'Well then, I'll phone a garage and tell them to come and fix the car. And then I'll ring Todd and ask him to come and get me out of here.'

Verna smiled up at me, a thin smile full of hate, and I felt suddenly afraid. 'You do that, honey,' she said quietly. 'You go ahead and call.'

I stared at her, and then turned and went inside. But I knew before I picked up the phone that the line would be dead. And I was right.

When I put the receiver down, I turned and found Verna standing in the doorway, smiling at me. 'So the phone isn't working?' she said. 'Now isn't that just too bad. I guess you'll just have to stay here a little longer, after all. Whether you like it or not.'

I swallowed hard and said, 'It certainly looks that way.' My heart was pounding like a pile-driver and I couldn't stop my hands from trembling. I knew I was trapped. I had to stay at the house whether I liked it or not. Unless I walked out. Unless I went to the next house and asked to use their phone. Unless I walked up to the highway and hitched a lift.

'I – I think I'll go for a walk,' I said, edging towards the front door.

'In this heat? Don't be crazy.' Verna didn't move but her eyes were watchful. 'We'll just spend a quiet day here together. Same as usual. Okay?'

'Okay,' I said. 'I'll – I'll go and sit on the beach for a while.'

'Good idea. I'll come with you.'

Verna kept by my side all that day. Our stretch of beach was private and no one else used it. Anyway, who would believe that I was being kept at the house against my will? But I knew that if I tried to leave, Verna would stop me. I must try and keep calm. Sooner or later someone would come and find us. I must just keep calm, that's all.

It was late in the afternoon when Verna suggested we go for a swim together. I shrugged and waited while she went inside to change. She reappeared after a while, looking surprisingly slim and youthful in a plain one-piece swimsuit.

'I don't know why you're in such a hurry to leave the beach,' she said to me dreamily, as we walked towards the water's edge. 'Won't you miss the sea?'

'I might,' I said, and then I squealed as a cool wave lapped my legs. 'But I want to get back to Saxonwood.'

'Saxonwood's mine,' Verna said then in a hard voice that I scarcely recognised. I looked at her in surprise as I walked on into the sea and then I stopped short as she suddenly gripped me by the arm and said again, 'Saxonwood's *mine*. You've no right to it. No right at all.'

'But my father,' I began. 'My father left –'

She gave a loud sharp laugh. 'He didn't know what he was doing, the stupid fool. Leaving the house to *you*, a child he'd hardly seen, someone who doesn't know the house, doesn't love it – ' She gave me a look so full of hatred that I gasped out loud. 'You don't deserve to have it. And you *won't* have it. I won't let you sell it. I won't *let* you!'

'But I'm not going to sell it!' I shouted desperately. 'I wouldn't dream – '

'*I heard you say that you would*!' Her grip on my arm tightened. I tried to get free but she was surprisingly strong.

'I promise you that I'm not going to sell Saxonwood!' I gasped. 'Please believe me!'

Her grasp relaxed then and I pulled my arm away. We stood in the surf for a moment, staring at each other. And it was then that I realised the truth.

'It was you, wasn't it?' I said. 'Following me in the Cadillac, trying to get into my room. You tried to kill me by forcing us off the road.'

Verna smiled grimly. 'Not me,' she said. 'Sam. He did all that. He'll do anything for money, that man. I was just trying to frighten you, frighten you away.'

'But why? *Why*?'

'I won't let you take Saxonwood from me,' she said, and then she grabbed my arm again in a grip like steel. I staggered and fell backwards into the sea, and she fell with me, on top of me. We struggled for a moment as wave after wave washed over us, and then I felt her hands pressing down on my head, pushing me down, down. I tried to shout but my mouth filled with water and all I could feel was a great weight on my chest and a roaring blackness in my head that grew louder and louder . . .

Chapter Ten

I know I struggled because I remember lashing out and hitting someone with my fists but I seemed powerless against the weight on my chest and the roaring darkness in my head. And then, suddenly, the pressure lifted and I struggled to the surface, gasping and spluttering and sobbing with fear. I struck out with my fists again, aware of hands trying to hold me back. A wave washed over me, filling my eyes and mouth with water, and I choked and fell, my arms and legs flailing wildly. Then the arms found me again and I fought feebly to escape them until I realised suddenly that they were holding me and lifting me and that a voice in my ear was saying, 'Laura! Laura, it's okay. You're safe now. Everything's okay.'

'Don't,' I groaned. 'Leave me alone. Please . . .' Then the roaring mist in my eyes and ears began to clear and I realised that I was standing now, with my head resting on someone's chest, and that strong arms were holding me gently but firmly. I looked up and saw, far above, a single seagull drifting in a brilliant blue sky. And then, closer, looking down at me, a face I knew so well.

'Hi!' said Jake. 'I hope you don't mind my dropping in like this.'

I stared at him for a moment, not knowing whether to laugh or cry. Then he lowered his face to mine and gave me a long salty kiss that took my breath away and stopped me from doing either.

After that, we staggered up the beach together and I remember looking round wildly for Verna and saying, 'Where is she? She tried – '

'It's okay.' Jake's arms tightened round me. 'Verna's in no state to harm anyone. Todd's in the house with her now.'

'Todd's here too?'

Jake nodded. 'I called him this morning because I was missing you and I wanted to come out and see you but I didn't know the address. And he told me that he and his mother were worried because the phone here was dead and because Verna had been acting pretty strange the last few weeks. So we came out here together to make sure everything was okay.'

'And found Verna trying to kill me,' I said bitterly. By now we had reached the house and were climbing the stairs to the deck. I could hear the sound of someone sobbing inside and I guessed that it was Verna. 'I don't want to go into the house,' I said to Jake. 'I'll wait here until it's time to go back.'

'It's time now,' he whispered. 'Todd will stay here with your aunt until an ambulance arrives. I'm driving you home.'

'In the Beetle?'

He nodded. 'You were right, Aunt Ethel changed her mind. But I've got strict instructions to stay away from large black Cadillacs.'

This time I was delighted to see Saxonwood when at last Jake's little purple car lurched up the drive between the familiar green velvet lawns. I knew now that the house was safe, that it held no danger for me.

Jessica was waiting for us on the terrace and she held out her arms to greet me. 'Oh, Laura, we were so worried,' she said. 'Are you okay? What happened?'

I told her all I knew and then Jake described what he had seen when he and Todd arrived at the house. They had found it empty, of course, but when they stepped out onto the deck they had seen two figures struggling in the surf, seen Verna forcing me under . . .

'Oh, no,' Jessica groaned. 'How dreadful! And it's all my fault. I should never have allowed you to go with her.'

'You tried to stop me,' I said. 'You tried very hard to stop me. But I wouldn't listen. I was scared –' I stopped, knowing how stupid my suspicions seemed now. Then I went on, 'I thought *you* were trying to kill me. So that you could get Saxonwood back.'

Jessica let out a great whoop of laughter. 'Oh, Laura, if only you knew,' she said. 'I hate this house, I always have. Todd and I only moved in here because your father wouldn't leave it. But Verna, of course, was crazy about the place. Literally crazy.'

'Crazy enough to kill for it,' Jake said.

Jessica nodded. 'She's always been strange but your father's death really hit her hard, Laura. And then when you said you were going to sell Saxonwood, she really went bananas.'

I shivered, remembering the wild staring look in Verna's eyes and then the pitiful sobbing coming from the beach house as Jake and I left that evening.

'I've been so stupid,' I said slowly. 'I really thought *you* wanted to get rid of me.' And I told Jessica about the conversation between her and Todd that I'd overheard on my first afternoon at Saxonwood.

'We were talking about Verna,' she said. 'I had a suspicion that she'd cause trouble. I really felt she'd try to harm you because the house is now yours. And she did, of course, with Sam's help.' She came over then and hugged me. 'But it's all over now, Laura. Try and forget about the bad times and enjoy the rest of your vacation. Forget that the last few days ever happened.'

I did try to forget but it wasn't easy. Jake and I spent wonderful days together in the weeks that followed but at night, alone in my room at Saxonwood, the memories returned and I would wake screaming from nightmares about gigantic black cars forcing me down under green choking water.

But the dreams ended after a while and with them my time in California. Jake and I spent our last day together on the beach at Santa Monica but it wasn't really our last day because he'd be returning to London in the autumn and we'd see each other again then.

'See you at the airport,' I whispered, as we kissed goodnight in the front seat of the Beetle.

'I'm sure going to hate waving goodbye to you,' he said, stroking my hair. 'But it'll only be for a few weeks. Then we'll be together again.'

I smiled happily as his arms held me tight and close.

The next morning, I said goodbye to Maria and the rest of the staff and then went in search of Jessica. She was waiting for me outside on the sunlit terrace, by the purple oleander bush. 'Come back and see us soon,' she said, taking my hands in hers. 'Don't think too badly of us because of what happened.'

'I won't,' I said, then, 'I'm going to miss Saxonwood.'

'And we're going to miss *you*,' she smiled. 'Why not come and spend Christmas with us? We'd love another visit from you. And next time there'll be no – '

'There'll be no Verna here to spoil things,' I finished quickly.

Jessica nodded sadly. 'The doctors say she'll need care for a long time to come.'

I shivered as I remembered that terrible afternoon at Malibu. Then I pushed the memory from my mind and turned to take a last long look at Saxonwood.

Todd drove me to the airport in his Peugeot, back down the glittering boulevards of Beverly Hills and along the crowded freeways that soared above the city. We didn't say much; perhaps we were both remembering another journey we'd made together, side by side in the black Cadillac on my first day in California.

'Well, farewell, cousin dear,' he said at last, when the time came for me to board my plane. I was worried because there was no sign of Jake and so I didn't hear what he said at first. 'Farewell,' he repeated, then, 'It's a pity we didn't get to know each other better, Laura. But I guess I didn't stand much of a chance with Jake Shannon around. Where is he, by the way? Shouldn't he be here to see you off?'

'Oh, don't worry about him,' I said lightly. 'Maybe he got held up on the freeway. Goodbye, Todd.'

He didn't say anything. Instead he took me suddenly

into his arms and gave me an enormous hug that took my breath away. For one brief moment I forgot about Jake – all that seemed to matter was the touch of Todd's cheek against mine and his strong arms holding me tight. Then I sighed, and pushed him gently away.

'See you at Christmas,' I said. 'Maybe.'

I gazed for the last time into the mocking blue eyes and then I kissed him lightly on the cheek before turning away.

As the plane lifted at last into the clear blue sky, I leaned across the empty seat beside me for a last look at the gleaming freeways, the billboards and palms and small houses stretching into haze, and the great blue-green Pacific fringed with surf and beach. Then, at last, the bright colours of the city blurred and vanished behind cloud.

'Excuse me, ma'am, is that seat taken?'

I looked up, startled, and then my surprise melted into joy as Jake slipped into the seat beside me.

'I hope you don't mind my dropping in like this,' he said solemnly, 'but I decided that I'd rather spend the rest of the summer with you in London than without you in LA. How do *you* feel about that?'

'Come here,' I said, as I drew his face towards mine. 'Come here, and I'll tell you.'

But we didn't say anything at all for a very long time.

ARROW AD B23 —

More Beaver Books

On the following pages you will find some other exciting Beaver Books to look out for in your local bookshop

BEAVER BOOKS FOR OLDER READERS

There are loads of exciting books for older readers in Beaver. They are available in bookshops or they can be ordered directly from us. Just complete the form below and send the right amount of money and the books will be sent to you at home.

☐ THE RUNAWAYS	Ruth Thomas	£1.99
☐ COMPANIONS ON THE ROAD	Tanith Lee	£1.99
☐ THE GOOSEBERRY	Joan Lingard	£1.95
☐ IN THE GRIP OF WINTER	Colin Dann	£2.50
☐ THE TEMPEST TWINS Books 1–6	John Harvey	£1.99
☐ YOUR FRIEND, REBECCA	Linda Hoy	£1.99
☐ THE TIME OF THE GHOST	Diana Wynne Jones	£1.95
☐ WATER LANE	Tom Aitken	£1.95
☐ ALANNA	Tamora Pierce	£2.50
☐ REDWALL	Brian Jacques	£2.95
☐ BUT JASPER CAME INSTEAD	Christine Nostlinger	£1.95
☐ A BOTTLED CHERRY ANGEL	Jean Ure	£1.99
☐ A HAWK IN SILVER	Mary Gentle	£1.99
☐ WHITE FANG	Jack London	£1.95
☐ FANGS OF THE WEREWOLF	John Halkin	£1.95

If you would like to order books, please send this form, and the money due to:
ARROW BOOKS, BOOKSERVICE BY POST, PO BOX 29, DOUGLAS, ISLE OF MAN, BRITISH ISLES. Please enclose a cheque or postal order made out to Arrow Books Ltd for the amount due including 22p per book for postage and packing both for orders within the UK and for overseas orders.

NAME ....

ADDRESS ....

....

Please print clearly.

Whilst every effort is made to keep prices low it is sometimes necessary to increase cover prices at short notice. Arrow Books reserve the right to show new retail prices on covers which may differ from those previously advertised in the text or elsewhere.

JOAN LINGARD

If you enjoyed this book, perhaps you ought to try some of our Joan Lingard titles. They are available in bookshops or they can be ordered directly from us. Just complete the form below and enclose the right amount of money and the book will be sent to you at home.

☐ MAGGIE 1: THE CLEARANCE	£1.99
☐ MAGGIE 2: THE RESETTLING	£1.99
☐ MAGGIE 3: THE PILGRIMAGE	£1.95
☐ MAGGIE 4: THE REUNION	£1.95
☐ THE FILE ON FRAULEIN BERG	£1.99
☐ THE WINTER VISITOR	£1.99
☐ STRANGERS IN THE HOUSE	£1.95
☐ THE GOOSEBERRY	£1.95

If you would like to order books, please send this form, and the money due to:
ARROW BOOKS, BOOKSERVICE BY POST, PO BOX 29, DOUGLAS, ISLE OF MAN, BRITISH ISLES. Please enclose a cheque or postal order made out to Arrow Books Ltd for the amount due including 22p per book for postage and packing both for orders within the UK and for overseas orders.

NAME ....

ADDRESS ....

....

Please print clearly.

Whilst every effort is made to keep prices low it is sometimes necessary to increase cover prices at short notice. Arrow Books reserve the right to show new retail prices on covers which may differ from those previously advertised in the text or elsewhere.

ACTIVITY BOOKS

If you enjoy making and doing fun things, perhaps you ought to try some of our exciting activity books. They are available in bookshops or they can be ordered directly from us. Just complete the form below and enclose the right amount of money and the books will be sent to you at home.

☐ THINGS TO MAKE IN THE HOLIDAYS	Steve and Megumi Biddle	£1.99
☐ CRAZY COOKING	Juliet Bawden	£2.25
☐ CRAZY PUPPETS	Delphine Evans	£1.95
☐ THINGS TO MAKE FOR CHRISTMAS	Eric Kenneway	£1.95
☐ THE PAPER JUNGLE	Satoshi Kitamura	£2.75
☐ SPRING CLEAN YOUR PLANET	Ralph Levinson	£1.75
☐ HOW TO MAKE SQUARE EGGS	Paul Temple and Ralph Levinson	£1.50
☐ COACHING TIPS FROM THE STARS: SOCCER	David Scott	£1.99
☐ FREAKY FASHIONS	Caroline Archer	£1.95

If you would like to order books, please send this form, and the money due to:
ARROW BOOKS, BOOKSERVICE BY POST, PO BOX 29, DOUGLAS, ISLE OF MAN, BRITISH ISLES. Please enclose a cheque or postal order made out to Arrow Books Ltd for the amount due including 22p per book for postage and packing both for orders within the UK and for overseas orders.

NAME ....

ADDRESS ....

....

Please print clearly.

Whilst every effort is made to keep prices low it is sometimes necessary to increase cover prices at short notice. Arrow Books reserve the right to show new retail prices on covers which may differ from those previously advertised in the text or elsewhere.

BEAVER BESTSELLERS

You'll find books for everyone to enjoy from Beaver's bestselling range—there are hilarious joke books, gripping reads, wonderful stories, exciting poems and fun activity books. They are available in bookshops or they can be ordered directly from us. Just complete the form below and send the right amount of money and the books will be sent to you at home.

☐	THE ADVENTURES OF KING ROLLO	David McKee	£2.50
☐	MR PINK-WHISTLE STORIES	Enid Blyton	£1.95
☐	FOLK OF THE FARAWAY TREE	Enid Blyton	£1.99
☐	REDWALL	Brian Jacques	£2.95
☐	STRANGERS IN THE HOUSE	Joan Lingard	£1.95
☐	THE RAM OF SWEETRIVER	Colin Dann	£2.50
☐	BAD BOYES	Jim and Duncan Eldridge	£1.95
☐	ANIMAL VERSE	Raymond Wilson	£1.99
☐	A JUMBLE OF JUNGLY JOKES	John Hegarty	£1.50
☐	THE RETURN OF THE ELEPHANT JOKE BOOK	Katie Wales	£1.50
☐	THE REVENGE OF THE BRAIN SHARPENERS	Philip Curtis	£1.50
☐	THE RUNAWAYS	Ruth Thomas	£1.99
☐	EAST OF MIDNIGHT	Tanith Lee	£1.99
☐	THE BARLEY SUGAR GHOST	Hazel Townson	£1.50
☐	CRAZY COOKING	Juliet Bawden	£2.25

If you would like to order books, please send this form, and the money due to:

ARROW BOOKS, BOOKSERVICE BY POST, PO BOX 29, DOUGLAS, ISLE OF MAN, BRITISH ISLES. Please enclose a cheque or postal order made out to Arrow Books Ltd for the amount due including 22p per book for postage and packing both for orders within the UK and for overseas orders.

NAME ....

ADDRESS ....

....

Please print clearly.

Whilst every effort is made to keep prices low it is sometimes necessary to increase cover prices at short notice. Arrow Books reserve the right to show new retail prices on covers which may differ from those previously advertised in the text or elsewhere.